Hired Out

by Cathy Moore

"Hired Out," by Cathy Moore. ISBN 978-1-951985-47-9 (softcover); 978-1-951985-48-6 (eBook).

Don, my North Star

Foreword

Here is a story that honors a slave girl in Lexington, Kentucky before the Civil War. Not much is known of her because slaves were rarely mentioned, much less written about. This girl, named America, touched Kentucky history by giving birth to Isaac Burns Murphy, a nationally acclaimed racehorse jockey. Consideration of her ambition, intelligence, strength, and grace in a white-ruled society might explain his success.

Chapter 1
Catherine

"THEY PUT HER IN A BOX. Like a china doll. She was, oh so still … and white. Her face was not painted as a doll's would be, and her eyes were closed as if she were sleeping. But her mouth was set … and her hair was perfectly arranged." Catherine twitched, then jerked her head from side to side. "I remember wondering if they would put her away somewhere and bring her out later-and she could walk and talk and laugh again…" Her melancholy emerged with the memories.

America, well-behaved, had not interrupted Catherine who was five years younger. Mindful to keep the niece of Mistress Henrietta occupied with pleasant thoughts, America sought a distraction for this girl. "Miss Catherine, there's a vision to behold." America nodded in the direction of a green-trimmed carriage pulled by a matching pair of chestnut horses, rolling down Mill Street. "See how proud the horses look with their necks arched and the harness polished to a luster."

Catherine followed America's gaze to study the matched set. "I know those horses! They are twins, foaled at Grandfather's farm. They match in color. Even the white markings on their legs are the same."

"Twins, Miss Catherine?" America inquired.

1

"I first saw them when they were only a few months old. Aunt Mary and Uncle John took me out one afternoon after Mother passed away." Catherine sighed and shook herself, allowing a few auburn ringlets to escape from her blue and white bonnet. Sitting in the yard of the big house, Catherine's grief was never far away.

America tried to bring Catherine back to the present. "They are full grown now and look right smart, trained up to be a team for that fancy brougham."

"They probably looked out for each other when they were weanlings." Catherine did not respond to America's statement. As a white mistress, she did not consider the comments of a black servant important enough to address. She continued with her own thoughts. "I remember them squealing and crying when their dam was taken away. They charged around the paddock together, searching for her. Even though they were just foals, I felt their fear and panic, just as I did when they took Mother away."

"Well, Miss Catherine, could you tell me about your mother?" America had orders to draw Catherine away from her sadness, an impossible task. As a newly hired servant, she had to obey instructions, confusing as they were.

Her first day at the big house, America had been introduced to Catherine as her personal maid. Besides learning the rules and procedures of the household, she found that her primary responsibility was to see after this troubled niece of Mistress Henrietta. Catherine and her brother JW had returned to Hopemont three months ago from Frankfort where they lived with their Aunt Mary and Uncle John Hanna. The siblings had adjusted to life in the bustling Morgan household.

America sidestepped Catherine's heartache. "I'm sure you had happy memories of her."

Catherine turned toward America recognizing the attempt to lighten the conversation, a strategy used many times in her young life. She noticed that her dusky-skinned servant was watchful, resourceful, and mannerly. To Catherine's mind, America had a lot to learn and definitely needed to be put in her place: a servant does not ask for information about a departed parent. Straightening her bonnet and smoothing her dress to look the part of a high-born mistress, she began a litany of family lineage just as a proud horse owner would recite the pedigree of a favored equine.

"Mother was one of twelve children born to John Wesley Hunt. He was a good businessman, horse breeder, and a prominent citizen of Lexington. He built this house and named it Hopemont." Catherine peered at America to watch her reaction. And leaning toward her servant with a knowing smile, she stated, "Using slave labor and buying and selling Negroes is how he made money, besides his investments. Why, Mother's sister, Mistress Henrietta, has at least a dozen house slaves, like yourself, now, just to manage Hopemont."

With a blank look on her face, America remained unmoved. Catherine had purposely goaded her. Although churning with sadness at the thought of so many black lives wrapped around forced labor, she knew the necessity of presenting a calm expression if she wanted to remain a servant in this household. *Some of those slaves could teach me how to behave around the family, if they decide to help me.* "Hopemont? What a nice name for this beautiful house."

Catherine turned to peer at America again. She had been taught to ignore worthless statements of approval made by a servant. *After all, what knowledge does a slave have to form an opinion?* Voicing a judgment-however small-is not in the realm of correct behavior for a maidservant. Even though America's comment seemed genuine, Catherine chose to sniff at the remark.

"We lived in Louisville where Daddy..." Catherine was startled at the sudden clamor and shrieks coming

3

from the back of Hopemont house. Her brother rushed into view, along with cousins Thomas and Key. "Well, JW, you all don't need to come galloping around the corner. Please announce yourself first. That's the proper way."

"Good afternoon, Sister," the boy addressed her, as the two other boys about his age nodded. A bit out of breath and straining to put on a serious face, he paused as his adult cousin joined them. "I am faster on two feet than John is, pretending to have four feet."

"Why, JW?" Catherine knew the older, taller man would win in an even footrace.

"We were playing men against horse," her brother had to explain.

"But, you'd lose in a real race against a thoroughbred, my man," a deep voice countered. "Good afternoon, cousin." John Hunt Morgan lowered his six-foot frame into the garden bench, showing his good manners and patience with his younger relatives. John's young brothers departed to play in the garden with their newly crafted slingshots. After a moment to adjust his hat, John noticed America who stood very still behind Catherine's chair. "Catherine, is she your new girl?"

"Well, yes and no," Catherine slowly answered. "She was hired to help in the house, but Aunt Bette asked for her to be my girl. Aunt Henrietta agreed that she will work part of the time as a house servant and part of the time as my maid."

"What is her name?" JW asked, realizing that she wasn't much taller than he and Catherine.

"America. She is called America." Catherine gave a little smile as if sharing an amusing secret.

"America? I've never heard anyone called that." JW was confused.

"My Uncle Alexander's wife is named America. Of course, she is a real aunt, not like our Aunt Bette. And, I do believe there is a real good bay racehorse named

4

Lexington. He is darker in color." John offered, with a smile. "His sire was Boston. Place names. Somebody must have been thinking big when they named this girl." He turned to address America. "Do you like your name?"

"Yes, Sir," America replied, looking down at Catherine's chair. *Why is he talking to me?*

"Do you like your work here?" John looked her up and down.

Does he care? Or is he just being masterful? "Yes, Sir. I think I will." America explained further. "Since my master hired me out just yesterday I will do my best to make him proud."

"Now, my sister Henrietta... ," John was still thinking of names.

"Who is our cousin Tommy... ," Catherine turned to instruct JW.

"Was first nicknamed Tammy," John Hunt Morgan continued, serving as an authority on family connections.

"To tell the difference between Aunt Henrietta and her daughter Henrietta." Catherine seized the chance to educate America in the family relationships. "But that name sounded too much like 'Mammy' and we couldn't have that. So she became Tommy, which seems to fit."

JW politely listened to all the explanations but was not drawn into the name justifications.

"You will have to wait until fall to meet Tommy." John looked around. "She will liven up the household when she gets back from visiting Aunt Theodosia in St. Louis. I wonder if she misses us as much as we miss her."

Chapter 2
Hopemont

CATHERINE AND JW HAD MOVED with their mother to
Lexington from Louisville eight years ago. Already
suffering with consumption, Anna Hunt Reynolds had
come back to die in her family home. She brought her
children with her so that her siblings and Aunt Bette, their
childhood nurse, would care for them when she passed
away.

"Mother wanted to come back to Hopemont,"
Catherine explained to America the next day. "That
stupid, ignorant mammy in Louisville would separate JW
and me from Mother when she had those coughing fits.
We were only trying to help her get her breath!" Catherine
gazed at America.

"You must have felt helpless." America sympathized.
She thinks the black servant did not know as much about
nursing as she did.

"Besides, Lexington has better doctors and the latest
medical care," Catherine stated this fact as if she was the
one who made the decision. "Aunt Bette helped all she
could and we were allowed to be with Mother at any time.
We would play outside with her: hide the thimble,
checkers. What I loved most was listening to the stories
Mother made up as we played with our dolls. JW was

6

usually off playing hide-and-go-seek with Thomas and Key and the black house boys. The worst part was when Mother just stayed in bed because she was too weak." Catherine shook her head and frowned. "Aunt Bette tried to ease Mother's sickness, but it was too late. She stayed with Mother, singing lullabies and propping up her shoulders when the blood came with the coughs."

America sighed in pity for the girl. *But, my own mama would not have any nurse to help her die. We will go quickly. No doctor would come to our home, even though Papa is white. No doctor would come to help a sick black woman. Color decides.* America had listened politely and smiled, wondering if she would ever be as kind as Aunt Bette. "It is good that Aunt Bette was there for your mother. And, I am glad to be of service to you," she added.

"Oh, don't be so formal, America. The other girl who helped me was formal-distant-and all too slavish, if you ask me." Catherine paused and laughed, considering the slave she had just described as slave-like. Serious on the subject, she stated, "I want to be like a normal girl, with a friend, not the object of a fawning Negro like Hattie in Frankfort. Even though Aunt Mary and Uncle John are our guardians, they don't have any children of their own, just house servants. I hope JW and I can stay here for a long time with all the Morgans, in this house."

America was silent. *They want me to be her companion, like a friend. If it turns out that Catherine and I do not like each other, I will have to pretend to be her friend. Mama would tell me to just get along-to be safe. We have no choice.* She gave Catherine a weak smile. "Friends multiply the good in life and divide the evil. My mama once told me that."

"That's what I want: someone who is cheerful." Catherine looked down to think about her mother and how contented she had been around her. With a gulp, she said, "Stories in books can carry me away and make me happy. I love to read and memorize quotes."

"Yes." America's eyes sparkled. "And, I would love to make friends with books and learn how to read. Maybe you could teach a new friend," putting her hand on her chest to indicate herself, "how to read and we could make each other happy." Her broad smile lit up her face.

Catherine's white face turned pink with excitement as she too realized that a pleasant adventure had just begun.

Chapter 3
Kidnapped

CATHERINE WAITED IN THE PANTRY FOR AMERICA. She peered out the window near the servants' door, impatient to see her companion appear. As custom dictated, America would climb the few steps on the side porch leading to the door and then knock for entry.

This day, Catherine swung open the door just as America arrived. The dusky-skinned girl's hand was raised to knock. She stepped back in surprise.

"America, where were you yesterday?" Catherine blurted, with no words of greeting or acknowledgement of her arrival.

Aunt Bette stood up from the pantry rocking chair. She was small in stature, but exuded strength and health. Putting her hands on her hips, she stated, "Hired servants are to come for work every day. They do not get a day off." Her scold was as mild as her face appeared, but her stance left no doubt of her authority.

"Good morning, Miss Catherine... and Aunt Bette," America looked tired.

"Well, why didn't you come? I was expecting you!"

America gave a weak smile. "I was kidnapped."

Catherine's jaw dropped, and her eyes enlarged with a look of disbelief. Folding her arms across her chest, Aunt

Bette stood in quiet contemplation of the tawny-skinned girl at the door. Confused, Catherine asked, "But, but, but, here you are. How can you be kidnapped and be here with me?"

"I got away from him. He was distracted, and I escaped."

Catherine took a good look at America as her servant girl walked into the pantry: hair in place, clean dress, no visible cuts or bruises. But she saw a melancholy in her servant's eyes. America looked glum.

"Oh, America." Catherine fought for breath, as reality arrived with America's sad gaze. "What happened?"

"I was kidnapped." America looked down at her hands. She swallowed twice. She looked around the pantry. "I was walking down Second Street yesterday morning, coming here. The buildings were still in shadows, and I was not paying attention to my surroundings. I felt an arm around my middle, lifting me off the pavement. I smelled tobacco spit and whiskey."

Catherine sat down suddenly on a chair nearby. "America, I am so sorry."

"I realized: someone grabbed me," America continued, standing just inside the door. "I yelled for Master Murphy-he was not far away. But the man's arm tightened, and he clamped his other hand on my face. He did not say anything."

"Oh, oh, oh!" Catherine sputtered. "What did he look like?"

America shrugged. "He was behind me," she said. "But he was tall, strong enough to pick me up, and his long gait gave him an advantage."

"Slave stealer." Aunt Bette uttered the words as a sign of verifying America's situation.

"What did you do?" Catherine motioned for America to sit. Cook, overhearing America's words, stopped her food preparation to listen. She finally turned toward

America as one would face a new day, unsmiling and unsure what the future would bring.

America remained standing and smiled proudly. "I kicked him as hard as I could. Of course, it was a backward kick, so it wasn't as strong as I could have done. I pounded against his arm." She acted out her words.

"Did your master hear you?'

"No, the man had covered my mouth," America said. "His hand muffled my screams, so all that came out were yelps."

"Oh, America, how did you ever get away?"

"Well, I did what I could," said America. "I beat on his arms and scratched his hand. He conveyed me to a secluded spot-that alley near Market Street. There was a horse-drawn carriage."

"He was going to take you away in his carriage!" Catherine clapped her hand to her mouth to hide her quivering lips. Her wide-open eyes, though, communicated her fright. *America could have disappeared with no trace. I would never have seen her again!*

"I knew no one would be coming to my aid. I had to do something immediately or die as a fancy girl."

Aunt Bette realized that America was aware of what would happen to a kidnapped colored girl in Lexington. "This place is the center of slave business. Slave stealers bring their stock, and black traders come from miles around." She knew the harm.

"I set up a frantic howl. He was stealing me. And he was getting away with it. He kept a tight hold on my middle. The pressure left me breathless. Anger worked its way up to my mouth. I got ready to bite him."

"Like a horse!" Catherine interrupted.

"Yes, in all that terror, I thought of a trapped animal," replied America. She stopped to smooth her dress. "For a moment, I tried to imagine what a horse would do. But, when he saw my teeth, the man raised his arm, preparing to slap me. I ducked to avoid his hand, but he must have thought better of it."

America took a breath, and then continued. "I tilted and turned to get a close look at him. Miss Catherine, he had a diamond ring. He was dressed in a fashionable suit, had a fancy waistcoat, a gold pocket watch, and a stylish beaver hat. He is white and had a dark short beard, like a goat's. I wondered if his hat covered devil horns. I thought, 'Would a gentleman act like this?' He was holding me against my will. I realized that he was no gentleman, even though he looked the part."

"Was he a slave stealer?" Catherine echoed Aunt Bette's term, making the information her own. She tried to imagine what being kidnapped would involve, but, of course, she was not a slave to be stolen. The terror on America's face as she told her story forced Catherine to be thankful that as a white girl she was reasonably safe. She realized that if the slave stealer put America up for sale, he wouldn't make as much money if she looked battered. *That's why he didn't hit her.*

"Well, I wondered. But, surely, no one dressed so fine would grab me for profit. Then I remembered what Mama had told me: 'Do not fight someone who could bring harm to you. Make them think you are cooperating, and they will be easier on you.' So I decided to play along with him. I stopped struggling. He took his arm from my middle and compelled me to stand next to the carriage. It was positioned facing outward, ready for a quick departure."

"He had everything ready, and now that you had stopped fighting him, he must have been pleased," reasoned Catherine.

"Yes," said America. "He started talking, to convince me to climb into the carriage. He used flattery, saying he would be delighted to have me ride in his fine brougham." America scowled and looked away. "I knew better."

"He had a fine carriage for slaves?" Catherine asked. She looked over to Aunt Bette.

"No one would question such an elegant conveyance: only a white gentleman would use it. At least that is what I am guessing he thought. I looked around for help and pretended to be charmed by his words. I spoke kindly to him but with a loud voice to somehow raise an alarm."

"Well, did he force you into the carriage?"

"Yes," said America. She shook herself at the memory. "It was not easy for him. I continued my loud talk and took my time pushing against him as best I could. He had to pry my fingers off the door frame. But then I climbed into the carriage." Her face softened.

Catherine's eyes widened again, but no sound came. America read her lips: "Why?"

"I spied help coming," America stated.

"What! Who?"

America smiled for the first time. "Uncle Eli. He appeared from the back side of the brougham, and stood next to it as if inspecting it." She shook her head. "I must have jerked hard because the man's grip was like a vise." She touched the sore spot on her shoulder and winced.

"Oh, dear, America," said Catherine, anxious for the story to end. "What help could he offer? Is he your uncle? Is he black?" Cook eased herself into the rocking chair that Aunt Bette used, attending to America's words.

"He is black, but we are no relation. He is a friend of Master Murphy, and I knew he would do his best to get me away from that evil man." America cringed. "On Uncle Eli's slight signal, I stopped struggling and got into the carriage."

"What! Why?" Catherine was confused.

"I did not understand at the time, but I do trust Uncle Eli. Maybe he planned to drive the carriage away? Or was he just wanting to get me out of the reach of the kidnapper? I still do not know."

"Well, what happened next?" Catherine was getting impatient.

"Oh, the inside of the carriage was terrible." America stopped, a distressed look on her face. "Please, excuse..." She stepped back, put her hand to her mouth, and gagged. She turned to the door, then hesitated and took a deep breath. Catherine had remained where she was and waited for her servant to gain control of her terror. Aunt Bette and Cook did the same.

"Ahhh," America began again. "I am sorry. It cannot be as bad, compared to what others have had to endure. I am lucky to be here with you talking about what happened." She straightened up, smiled weakly, and continued. "The smell was what I first noticed. Then the darkness wrapped all around me. I heard the door lock click. The kidnapper had locked me inside like a prisoner. Uncle Eli greeted the man and began talking to him about the horse and carriage. 'A well-behaved horse and a fine carriage, just right for a gentleman such as yourself,' I heard him say. Then he seemed to pause and was very quiet. 'I believe this set was due back at the livery yesterday. I know it is contracted for use this evening.'"

"What?" Catherine interrupted.

"I figured out later that Uncle Eli's greeting was a charade. The man, my kidnapper, told Uncle Eli that he was mistaken: the horse and brougham belonged to himself. 'No explanations are necessary for the likes of you,' he said. 'But I am on my way home with my spirited servant.' Those were his words for me! Well, that was a lie." America glowered.

"Yes. You are *my* servant," said Catherine, acknowledging her superior status.

America ignored Catherine's statement. "They continued to discuss the set while I surveyed the inside of the carriage as best I could. The heavy curtains were drawn. I found manacles near the seat. And my foot banged against a chamber pot. I gasped for breath and then realized the pot had not been emptied recently. It was the smell. And…"

Aunt Bette defined what America saw. "That carriage was furnished to carry kidnapped slaves."

America nodded. "I sensed fear and sorrow in that coach. It was dark inside. Shackles were attached to the carriage frame. Slaves would not be allowed outside to relieve themselves, thus the chamber pot and the stench of vomit and waste. They probably were compelled to sit in the gloom, bound to the carriage."

"How terrible, America," said Catherine. "That would have happened to you."

"Not if I could help it," America replied. "I decided to collect myself and think about getting away. Some words came to me." She looked at Aunt Bette and Cook and then back at Catherine. "I made a chant: 'Well, well, Magic Spell, get me out of this prison cell.' I kept repeating those words over and over very softly, keeping the rhythm by opening and closing my fists." America demonstrated her jingle and movement. "I tested the handle of the carriage door opposite the one I entered. It gave way under the pressure of my hand! Either my chant worked or the man had failed to lock it!"

"Ah, that is how you escaped?" asked Catherine.

Cook had surveyed America's appearance and returned to her work, still listening intently. Aunt Bette, though, watched the effect of America's story on Catherine, whom she had faithfully shielded from unfortunate circumstances.

America shook her head. "I did not try right away. I waited for a good opportunity. They had begun to squabble. I nudged the curtains aside to see Uncle Eli position himself a short distance from the carriage." America acted out pushing at the curtains. "Did he see me? I do not know."

"Do you remember what they said?"

"Some of it." She deepened her voice in imitation of her kidnapper: 'I own this brougham and its contents. What right does a black have to accuse me of chicanery! Lazy, worthless, hell-raiser! Unhand me!' I remember that and thought this was my chance. Had Uncle Eli tried to stop him? I do not know. My mind was on getting away. I pushed the door and it opened a bit. I crouched low and twisted on my knees. My foot found the step that would carry me down to the ground, and I crept from the brougham like a prowling fox. Then standing, I found myself between a stack of timber and the carriage. The men's voices got louder and angrier. Short, dark-skinned Uncle Eli had moved closer to the shed beside the alley, away from Second Street. And the tall, white skinned man followed him. His height and build dwarfed Uncle Eli's small frame."

"Does Eli work with horses?" asked Catherine. "He sounds clever and resourceful."

"He is." America answered solemnly. She began tiptoeing movements. "I timed my footsteps to the voices of the men. Gradually, I came to the tethered horse. I stroked and patted its neck, allowing it to see and smell me. He let out a soft whinny. Blinkered and harnessed to the carriage, he was ready for flight. I patted him again, thankful for his quiet behavior. The men had retreated farther into the alley."

"Did you run as fast as you could then?" asked Catherine.

"I was going to, but then the kidnapper looked toward the carriage," replied America. "I was afraid he could run faster and would grab me again. So I stood still, trying to blend into the shape of the horse. Turning back, the man accused Uncle Eli of interfering with his property. But Uncle Eli said, 'You, sir, are interfering with the livery stable's lease contract. You need to either return the horse and carriage or pay for their use.' When I saw the two men circling each other, like cats getting ready for a fight, I fled."

"Hurrah!" exclaimed Catherine. "It gave you time to run down the street."

"To Mama." America hinted that the ordeal was frightful. "By the time I got home, I presented quite a sight: panting, crying, and favoring my hurt shoulder. Mama pulled me inside where I coughed, heaved, and got my breath."

"I can just imagine what you looked like," said Catherine, loving the suspense of the true story. "Your dress wrinkled and dirty, your hair out of place, and your stockings torn... "

"And, I was missing my shoes," America told her. "I am lucky to have a pair of Mama's clogs to wear today. Trying to get away yesterday, I ran out of one shoe, and then took off the other one so I could go faster. I hope never to see them again. When I told Mama that I was kidnapped, she started with the same questions you did." Telling Catherine about her unfortunate experience gave America courage. It also made her realize that Catherine could be kindhearted.

Aunt Bette intervened. "Now, Miss Catherine. You need to ready yourself for your lessons. America, you are to help Cook with the milk and churning." The story and explanations ended for the day. The roles of young lady and servant began again with Aunt Bette as the overseer.

The capable slave cook showed her sympathy for America, who understood that she did have an ally in the household. "I sure am happy that Eli came along when he did. Otherwise, you might be training right now as another fancy girl, instead of a good companion for Miss Catherine."

"Do you know Eli?" Curious, Catherine resumed her role of young mistress by questioning the servant.

"Yes, child," Cook smiled. "He is a good friend and a righteous champion.

Chapter 4
The Slave Trade

CATHERINE ENJOYED AMERICA'S STORY and reveled in the fact of its truth as supplied by her servant. She wanted to hear more.

"I wonder how Father would have reacted to someone kidnapping me." Catherine brought up the subject as the girls sat outside that afternoon, winding silk thread for her embroidery work. "I'm sure he would be angry and would stop at nothing to capture the man. Constables and the sheriff would track him down. It would take a brazen and foolhardy person to even dare to kidnap one of our family."

"Yes, Miss Catherine. You should feel safe to have many people look out for you." America stated the fact as comfort for the young mistress; however, her own situation was just the opposite. *Nobody would go running to find my kidnapper. Capturing a horse thief is more important than catching a slave stealer.* She frowned at the realization.

"Was your master angry?" Catherine saw America's sad, angry look. She was curious about America's family.

"Yes, Miss Catherine, he was." America stood up and acted out her description of Jeremiah. "He did not say a lot, but he whacked the kitchen table with the newspaper he carried, kicked at a chair, then shoved on his hat and stomped out the door. But when he returned, he had gotten control of his anger and showed a somewhat satisfied look."

America continued the story by imitating Jeremiah's voice. "Eli told me he had seen the kidnapper before, around the slave pens, and even in the crowds at the auctions." She hugged herself and swayed back and forth on her toes, acting out Jeremiah's words. "By his account, I figure the scoundrel is James McMillen, an agent of Lewis Robards."

"Robards. That name is familiar." Standing, Catherine brushed the silk lint from her skirt and peered upward. She did not know why she recognized the name of Lexington's well-known 'slave buyer'.

"I never want to see that Mister McMillan again." America whispered the words and swallowed at the lump in her throat. "It took me a long time to settle down. Master Murphy did not smile at all last evening, even when I said I was lucky to escape."

"I think your luck was courage in action," Catherine said. "Maybe the magic chant helped too. It has changed you."

"Maybe so," replied America. "Miss Catherine, I was about to be stolen and no one was coming to help. It made me angry. That man thought he could just carry me away-like picking an apple. Then when he and Uncle Eli started arguing over me, like a piece of property, it made me want to scratch their eyes out."

"America, you changed another way. For the better," said Catherine.

"Yes, seeing as I got away from him," America said. "I believe I can face terrors now."

"How is that?" asked Catherine.

"I survived," America said.

"And I am so glad you did. But there is a further change I'm happy about," said Catherine. "You are not formal with me as before. I like that we are becoming friends and share our thoughts. But, I notice that I'm still 'Miss Catherine."

"As a black servant, I will keep calling you 'Miss Catherine' because otherwise I would get in trouble. I consider you to be a friendly mistress, though." America told her. "I am glad you understand what happened to me."

"Yes." Catherine squeezed her arm. "We can talk like friends."

"I will keep using polite names and being respectful to white folk, even if they do not deserve it. That shows I know my manners. Mister McMillen looked and spoke like a gentleman." She paused. "He is not!" America raised her voice. "He is more like a..."

"Wolf in sheep's clothing," Catherine finished her thought with a smile, remembering that her mother said things like that.

America nodded. "Yes, Miss Catherine, he was like a wildcat on the prowl. Uncle Eli showed how to outsmart whites who want to do harm."

"How is that?" Catherine wanted to know.

"Kill them with kindness." America immediately realized she should not have uttered the phrase that slaves wished for their owners. But, if she and Catherine were going to be on friendly terms, she had to be honest.

A few days later, Jeremiah came home with news. "Robards is in trouble with the law again!" As the family sat down to their evening meal, he told them that the sheriff was in the process of selling Robards' slave business to satisfy his creditors. "And Mister James McMillen is now an agent for Washington Bolton, who sent him to Maysville. So, Merry, you need not look over your shoulder for that scoundrel."

"But Papa, there will be others to look out for." The thought of being kidnapped gave America the shivers. The gravy-and-biscuit supper became a knot in her middle.

"Wily slave trader that he is, McMillen would have learned to keep a distance from you. I think Uncle Eli's interception taught that lesson."

"Do you think he will use his carriage set in Maysville?" America could not rid herself of the frightening memory of the conveyance.

"Ahh, it was the carriage set that led me to discover that Robards was finally in deep difficulties. He went bankrupt. He had been sued too many times for his dishonest practices. Miss Catherine's cousin, John Hunt Morgan, had unpleasant business dealings with him. That horse and the carriage McMillen put you in, belonged to Robards! The sheriff sold it to pay off his debts." Jeremiah could not hide his amusement.

"Papa, why are you so happy about a slave trader getting out of debt? If I had my say, he would be locked away for the rest of his days-in his own slave jail."

"Merry, Merry, not contrary, who do you think bought the carriage set?"

"Oh, Papa. You did." America bowed her head. Then she bobbed it up to face him and to voice her fright. "I never want to get near that carriage. The inside is scary: I could feel the terror and the misery it held."

"On the contrary, Merry." Jeremiah looked straight at her. "We have already started to change the looks of it: taken out the shackles and the filthy chamber pot."

America put her hand to her mouth to control the gag. Then she raised a hand to stop him. "Papa, do not tell me more."

"Now, hear me out." Jeremiah became very earnest. "We are sanding down and varnishing all the woodwork inside and out: fitting it with new upholstery and curtains.

The ironwork will be reconditioned along with the driving tack. You will not recognize it because the outside paint will be a new color with trim to outline the body."

"You sound like a solicitor for your livery!" America paused. "And I guess you are!"

"You just wait to see what that carriage will become. Even Miss Catherine would want to take a ride in it."

America glanced at her mama who had a satisfied, proud look. "Papa, how is the horse that came with it?"

"That horse is healthy and cooperative." Her papa seemed pleased with his new purchase. "Robards took better care of it than he did the slaves he sold down the river."

Chapter 5
Responsibilities

AMERICA STEPPED AROUND HORSE EXCREMENT on Upper Street and dodged the shadows that lowered the temperature of the early morning air as she made her way to Hopemont, at the corner of Mill and Second Street. In the company of many Negro laborers on their way to work, she felt a sense of protection from slave catchers. The dawn's pink light provided her with a happy outlook: maybe today would bring some special news. Her steps were light and swift.

As usual, she was a bit early for her workday, but took comfort visiting with Cook and Aunt Bette. Owned by Mistress Henrietta herself, Aunt Bette, the children's longtime nurse and nanny, was the leader of household slaves. Because she lived upstairs in the servant quarters of the big house, her presence and knowledge allowed her to oversee the servants. Cook was hired out. She worked long days and shared kitchen duties with a helper. She had been leased to Master Morgan for many years. Her annual contract called for a small cash payment for herself in addition to the rental fee to her owner.

When the three house servants heard the ringing of the table bell, they knew that the family's breakfast was over. Mistress Henrietta used the silver hand bell as a signal to children and servants that morning chores should begin. America began clearing the table, and Cook immediately started preparations for the dinner meal.

Already dressed for school, Catherine came into the pantry. "Good morning, America. You need to learn the letters of the alphabet." She always came straight to the point when her contentment was in question.

"Good morning, Miss Catherine. I would love to learn the letters. It would put me on the path to reading!" America's eyes sparkled as she looked from Cook to Aunt Bette. *Here is the good news-a beginning of the chance to better myself! I cannot wait to tell Mama! But, first things first.* "I would like to know why you think I need to learn the letters." She had heard the words 'you need' from her young mistress a number of times before. It usually led to more work or uncomfortable circumstances.

"I want you to help me with my sampler. It is such a tedious job. I stopped working on it when JW and I came here. I had not forgotten about it, but no one seemed to push me to finish it. Now Mistress Dunham requires a second, more detailed sampler! Embroidery work takes up a lot of my time." Catherine smiled at the three slaves. Cook busied herself with food chores as Aunt Bette asked the obvious question.

"Do you mean to have America finish your sampler for you?"

"No, Aunt Bette." Catherine hesitated, gathering herself. "But, she could plan the spacing of the letters on the linen and suggest how to make them look tidy and cut away the silk threads if it doesn't go right and..." Catherine had already run out of possibilities-and excuses. "She is good at sewing."

"I will talk with Mistress Henrietta about this likelihood."

"She would just be learning the *letters*." Catherine's voice was tinged with a whine. America listened very intently, clasping her hands in respectful and hopeful silence.

"Now, you go on to school, Miss Catherine." Aunt Bette hinted at the need to be prompt. "Mistress Dunham will be checking your attendance, especially with the school year almost over." The black servant knew how to manipulate her young white charges toward proper behavior.

"I attend an *academy*, not a school, Aunt Bette." Catherine felt the need to put the well-loved slave in her place, as she turned to follow the enslaved woman's direction.

"It is for properly brought up young ladies. I would be in trouble if I allowed you to be late." Aunt Bette had a calm answer for her young mistress.

Catherine put on her school apron and gathered her slate and chalk and reader. She went out the side door with a goodbye smile for her maidservant.

America knew her duties by then. While Catherine attended the Lafayette Female Academy, she helped with kitchen chores, made sewing repairs, assisted with the hot ironing, and did various household cleaning work as needed. That day, she could hardly wait until Catherine returned in the afternoon.

"America, if Mistress Henrietta gives permission for Miss Catherine to teach you the letters, the two of you could sit here in the pantry for your lessons and work on the sampler. Cook will make space for you at the little table there under the window," Aunt Bette motioned. "We can keep an eye on you and maybe learn a little ourselves."

No wonder the Morgan children loved their Aunt Bette. She anticipated and accommodated the wishes of everyone, including America. The older slave shared a physical resemblance with America: they were both short and thin, although Aunt Bette was many skin shades darker.

26

"Thank you ever so much." The grin on America's face would not be extinguished that day. She could count on two allies in her quest for reading knowledge. As she picked up an empty water bucket for a trip to the cistern outside, she noticed a male servant at the side door. The package he shifted to free one hand to knock, was of a medium size, wrapped in heavy paper. America opened the door on Aunt Bette's command. The two young adults stared at each other.

"Why, Jerry. You have brought more books for Master Morgan." Aunt Bette validated her command of the household life by acknowledging the young black man's presence. "America, bring in the water for scrubbing. Then we will see what Jerry brought from Master Skillman."

"Yes. Maybe we can figure out some of the letters on each book blanket." America quickly glanced at Aunt Bette. She could hardly believe her good luck that morning. Miss Catherine had started plans for her reading education, and then this handsome servant boy appeared.

"Blanket??? There is no blanket," Jerry addressed America. "Ahhh, you mean *cover*! The books have covers. The pages are bound and protected by a cover, like a blanket. Yes. I can see how you would call it a blanket." His eyes twinkled. "And books can bring *comfort*." Now, he was playing with words.

But Jerry stopped talking: he had spoken more than his station allowed. His eyes, though, showed an appreciation for America's looks and for her limited perception of reading. The books were a set of adventure stories by Sir Walter Scott. Although Master Skillman had retired from the bookselling business, he still supplied favored customers with treasured reading materials. After America completed her water-bucket chore, Jerry showed her how to arrange the books in the bookcase of Master Morgan's office that had all the fixtures of a comfortable library.

"America. Is that your name?" Jerry paused, turning to leave.

"Yes. And you are called Jerry?" America wanted to make sure. *Huh. Jerry rhymes with Merry.*

Later that day, Mistress Henrietta paid a visit to the pantry. She brought embroidery supplies and asked America to show her needlework skills. Unhurried with the request, America exhibited a calm, respectful, capable appearance as she readied the materials. Explaining that she would embroider a small hill with the sun peeking over it on the linen to show the various stitches she knew, America selected the thread colors. The quick picture she created in thread signified the name of the dwelling: Hopemont.

America then stitched a small cat-like figure as an extra example of her proficiency. "And this, Mistress Henrietta, is…"

"A cat! For Catherine! How clever!" Surprised at her own swift recognition of the symbol and resulting heartening response, Henrietta turned the linen over to hide her enthusiasm. Upon examining the tidy backside of the embroidered piece, she nodded her satisfaction with America's work.

"Child. You are handy!" Aunt Bette was impressed. "Miss Catherine can learn a thing or two from you."

"This arrangement should be satisfactory. The work on Catherine's sampler must be her own, you understand." The mistress of the house was emphatic.

"Yes, Mistress Henrietta. I will help with the embroidery and teach her the stitches. I will need to learn the letters and words that she might want to put on the sampler. Miss Catherine seems willing to teach me those, with your permission." America took the opportunity to be forthright with her wishes to learn to read.

"All right. Aunt Bette will oversee your work." Henrietta glanced over to her favorite servant to confirm her additional responsibilities. She turned to America. "Now that Miss Dunham's academy year is nearly over, Catherine will have more time to spend on completing her sampler. It must be her needlework, not yours."

"Yes, Ma'am."

But life intervened.

Master Morgan died.

America knew his death would be soon because everyone spoke in hushed voices of his failing health and inability to come downstairs for meals. He spent most of his days reading the books sent from Abraham Skillman and delivered by Jerry. The *Waverly* novels by Sir Walter Scott depicted acts of courage and honor that brought comfort to the dying figurehead of the Hunt Morgan household. Catherine, herself an appreciative reader of Scott's works, was surprised to notice that Jerry could read.

Instructed to keep quiet and subdued near the sick room, America wondered how the master's death in the very room Catherine's mother had expired would affect her young mistress. Uppermost in her mind, however, was how Master Calvin's death would affect her status in the household.

"Things will change, Merry," Jeremiah told her on the morning of Calvin Morgan's burial. "I have your contract that Master Morgan signed. I expect Mistress Henrietta to honor it until September."

"The change has started. Aunt Bette already has me helping more with meals and housework. I overheard her talking with Miss Henrietta about Catherine's adjustment to Master Morgan's death."

When Mary and John Hanna stayed at Hopemont during Henrietta's time of mourning, arrangements were made for Catherine and JW to return to Frankfort at the beginning of the school year in the fall. Mary had decided that the children of their late sister Anna would benefit from the calm, quiet atmosphere of the Hanna home. JW would learn the habits and customs of business connections from John who was a prominent citizen of Frankfort. Catherine did not have a say about the move back. Friendship with a slave would not be a valid argument against the decision made by her well-meaning aunts.

"America, I will be going back to live with Aunt Mary and Uncle John in Frankfort." Catherine told her. "I will miss you. Your friendliness has helped me overcome the sadness of losing Mother. I regret that we will not share the reading lessons I had planned." She sighed.

America's sadness matched Catherine's. She did not consider herself a friend to the young mistress because they were not equals. She certainly thought of herself as a valued house servant, however, and that position would be in jeopardy. But, what America came to realize and lament, was that Catherine would not be present to teach her to read. Her usual response to any situation with Catherine, though, was to say something positive and hope for the best.

"Miss Catherine, we will have all summer to enjoy each other's company. You can begin your lessons with me as if we had all the time in the world. I just might surprise you by the time you have to leave. We can do the best with what we have."

Cook interrupted to remind the girls of America's duties. "Time is wasting, girl. This icy cream needs to be worked ever so lightly and those berries need your soft hand on the hulling." Cook expected her helper to keep up with the food preparation chores and be as hardworking as she was. She paused. "You'll be playing school only when Miss Catherine is here with us."

"Yes, Cook." America washed her hands and started to stir the cooled cream, vigorously preparing it to be returned to storage in the ice room. It would be brought up to the pantry for a final stirring and then placed in the china ice cream serving bowls in the dining room to accompany the fresh strawberries.

"Now, take that cream downstairs to get icy firm. It has to harden off considerably before we can bring it back up for dessert."

Later, Catherine quietly appeared in the pantry door and snatched a strawberry from the pile America had hulled. "Tasty. I like them best without the sugar glaze." She addressed America but spoke so that Cook could hear. "When you have finished here, come to the office room. Uncle Calvin's books are still there. Aunt Henrietta said I could pick some of them to keep."

"Yes, Miss Catherine." America, excited at the prospect of helping with the books, understood that her first responsibility now was to assist Cook.

The next day, Catherine collected in her bedroom all the things she would use for the lessons: scrap paper, quills, ink pot, rags, slate frames, chunks of limestone, and her old primary reading books. America carried the items down to the pantry and placed them in a basket near the table under the window, inspecting each piece as a treasure.

"Have you ever handled these things?" She asked Cook as she nodded toward the school supplies. America wondered at Cook's reading experience.

"Only when I was a chambermaid before I came here. Those pieces of limestone make a terrible mess. And, I have to watch that one of our boys doesn't carry off the good cutting knife to trim quills."

"I meant, do you know anything about reading?"

"Only that it is a powerful thing. Whites put great store in it. Why else would most of them guard against us black folk learning it?" Cook's reasoning was simple, realistic, and unfortunate.

"Well, yes. Reading and writing are powerful. And, from what I can tell, printed out, the words can be almost magical."

"Huh. What would be magical is if a book started flapping its covers like a butterfly or a bird and then carry you off away from here. That would be powerful. But I don't know about such things."

Chapter 6
Master and slave

READING WAS MAGICAL to those who did not know how. Cook, Aunt Bette, and almost all the slaves America knew could not read. It was a pleasant surprise to her that Jerry, owned by Abraham Skillman, was the exception. But because of his dark skin color, everybody recognized that he was a bonded servant. His skin was his identification. And America's status was ruled by the color of her skin. *Blacks were slaves, whites were free.* Color was important.

America's mulatto color could not be changed. She was a slave because Anne, her black mother, was the slave property of her white father, Jeremiah. America yearned to change her standing by learning to read, to no longer be viewed as an ignorant bit of chattel. Moreover, she had an advantage. Jeremiah Murphy, unlike most slave owners, loved her as any kindhearted parent would.

In the comfortable kitchen of Jeremiah's home on Upper Street, America had broached the subject of bettering herself with her Master Murphy before. The conversation recurred, as it had for many weeks, and

Jeremiah, ever the investor, considered the economic advantages of hiring out his own daughter.

"Merry, Merry, not contrary, how does your garden grow?" Jeremiah stepped through the kitchen doorway. It was their usual greeting-an English nursery rhyme they had modified on a whim. He waited for America's response.

"With silver bells, and magic spells, and bright colors all in a row." Their call and response never failed to make America smile, as did the pleasure of her papa's company.

"Merry, your smile illuminates this room." Having taught America the rhyme he had learned from his parents, he took great pride in her creative change of the words. He squeezed her wet arm. Turning to her mama, he doffed his hat and gave an exaggerated bow. "Good afternoon, Anne."

"Master Murphy." Her eyes twinkled, but she only nodded, dried her hands and arms, and then turned the only comfortable chair in the kitchen toward the fireplace for him.

Jeremiah hung his hat on a peg near the kitchen door and inspected the contents of the bean kettle in the fireplace before sitting down. He placed a newly folded newspaper on the well-used wooden table.

Anne set out the supplies for making cornbread. Then she dipped water from the bucket near the sink to fill the water kettle and swung it in place closer to the bright orange embers in the fireplace. Her movements were accomplished silently and efficiently. All was quiet. Peaceful. Warm.

"Merry, I am evaluating a house servant arrangement for you." Jeremiah studied America's labors and eyed Anne's reaction.

"Oh, yes, Papa." America stopped scrubbing on the washboard. "Have you any possibilities?" Her eyes became animated with expectation.

"Uncle Eli told me that Master Morgan of Hopemont is planning to hire a house girl. He suggested I look into it."

"He knows that I wish to be a house servant." America hinted at the short conversation she had with Eli Jordan.

"I will investigate what is needed and the terms of a hire." Jeremiah sighed at the prospect of sending America to work for the Morgans. It would give him more income, but Anne would be without their daughter's assistance with the laundry service.

"Thank you, Papa." America paused and then became serious as she pointed to herself and her mama. "We are your slaves?" She treated the statement as a question.

Jeremiah Murphy, surprised at his daughter's unexpected statement, countered with a question. "Child. You know the answer. What can I say?"

"The truth." America's face quivered.

"Yes, dear one," Papa frowned, waiting for inspiration. The afternoon blue sky had turned to evening gray. Suddenly, he got up from his chair and walked into the middle room, intent on changing his low-cut formal boots to more comfortable soft leather slippers for the evening.

Anne whispered to America. "Merry, your papa and I love each other. We love you." She cut through America's conjecture.

America faced her with a soft reply. "I want to be more than Papa's slave. I see black girls all around Lexington. Most appear to be wary or sad. How can you be a true person and still be a slave?" She kneaded the hem of the stained cotton dress in the warm soapy water.

That question begged for more explanation. Anne, intent on getting the wash done, wanted no interruptions of her quality, timely service. She glanced at her daughter.

With her hair braided up away from her tawny face and her small, slim body clothed in a worn osnaburg garment, America looked younger than she was. She splashed a soiled dress down into the clean smelling gray wash water in the wooden tub. Since the water had become a more-moderate temperature, she was able to search the depths of the wash tub for another garment. She stated the obvious: "You were a house girl when you were about my age. I have heard some of the stories."

"After you rinse this shirt in the blue water and wring it out, hang it outside to dry. I am going to let these other white shirts soak in the lye soap to get the stains out while I make a pot of tea for Master." Anne unrolled the sleeves of her work dress then poured the steaming water into the brown earthenware teapot. As the aroma of sassafras filled the humid kitchen, she set out the cups for tea. Her spotless, white head wrap made her appear taller. She wore it as much to keep her hair out of the way as a sign of her station in life: an impeccable, experienced laundress.

"Now, I will tell you more about my being a house girl." Anne paused to decide what to say. "My mama was owned by Miss Elizabeth. When she got married everything Miss Elizabeth owned, including your grandmamma, became the property of her husband. Mama had to do what he said. I was the child of Mama and Master Henry. Soon after I was born, I was put in with the other slave babies and raised by Mammy Lucy. When I was five years old, I was put to work in that house. I would turn the spit in the cooking fire, fetch hen eggs, and sweep the pathways outside the house, all things that would teach me to follow orders."

Having stirred the beans and salt pork that had been simmering since noon, she added a bit of seasoning in preparation for the evening meal. "My mama was sold away when I was around fourteen years old. I never saw her again. By then, I was old enough to learn how to be a house girl and maid: sewing, cleaning, washing, ironing, hair dressing, seeing after the white babies-anything the mistress told me to do. I learned quickly and figured out what was required." A frown wrinkled her brow, and her face hardened with memories.

Knowing that her mama had not explained the distress of working as a house servant, America waited. Staring out the window, Anne's face softened into a smile.

"I was about eighteen, and a Mister Murphy came to negotiate a sale."

"Papa." America nodded at Jeremiah as he reentered the room while she poured the steaming beverage. The hot tea served as a tonic for listening to Anne's history. She was impatient to get to the end of it but knew there was more pain to be told. America shrugged and gave words to her ambition. "I do not wish be a washerwoman for all my days! I want more than that. Being a house girl is a way out."

Unexpectedly, pride showed on Jeremiah's face as he nodded in Mama's direction. "Anne, you have taught her how to do laundry work, how to speak well, how to be kind, how to appear mannerly." Then Jeremiah turned to his daughter. "And, Merry, you want to rise above your station."

America frowned. "Yes. I do. That is what all of us are trying to do: Mama works hard to be known as a good laundress, you make business deals and own slaves." She sighed and then revealed her plan. "I want to be a house girl and learn to read."

"How is that going to happen?" Jeremiah's voice turned flat. "There is no school for colored girls." He knew that statement was inaccurate, but pressed on, understanding that America and Anne would not challenge him on the subject of black-and-white status in Lexington. Then he blurted the question. "How will reading help?"

"Well." America wrinkled her brow.

"I did not tell you of the harm that came." Anne's look mirrored America's. "A house girl must do everything a master says... " She stopped. Remembrance bubbled up to gurgle fear.

"Yes."

There was more. Anne tried to control her words. "I, uh..."

Jeremiah broke in. "There was no respect. No help. No reprieve."

"I was raped by Master Henry-more than once." Anne whispered the fact. Creases of pain and anger, smoothed away by tears and time, had returned.

America saw and understood the harm. Her hand flew to her mouth to hide her grimace of grief. Then, "Oh, Mama, you have carried that memory all these years!"

Jeremiah interrupted, hoping for a peaceful end to the explanation. "I came along. I was looking for a house girl."

"He bought me." America's mama smiled at the known fact.

"But, Mama, were you afraid?" America tried to imagine her mother as a girl in Master Henry's household and the idea of being sold to a stranger.

Jeremiah let the conversation continue without him. He occupied himself, studying the paper from the respite of his seat near the fireplace now that his comfort had been attended.

"Yes, Merry." Anne whispered, glancing at Jeremiah. "Was I going to be his fancy girl-or what? Turns out, I was lucky."

"Have you ever wanted to be free?" America murmured the question, although she was fairly sure of the answer.

"Yes, America." Her mama, looking down, softly spoke the truth. "But Master Murphy has made our life safe. As a colored woman out on my own, I would be prey for every slave catcher who saw me. I do not like being your papa's property because I have no say in what is to be. But, I am content with this life." She looked at Jeremiah and, in a clear voice, said, "I love him, and I love you."

Jeremiah looked up and nodded. "We fell in love about a year after I brought your mama to this house. Then you came along." Pride and satisfaction wreathed Jeremiah's face.

"Now my time has come." America claimed the moment.

Chapter 7
Seeking a way

ANNE NODDED. THE FROWN RETURNED. "Now, Merry. A house girl." She knew what was coming and would not question Jeremiah's plans to hire out their daughter. However, the discussion begged for clarification.

"If Mistress Morgan is looking to hire a house servant, I could fit right in. I already know how to do laundry. And, you've taught me sewing and embroidery work and how to help in the kitchen." Merry was excited at the prospect.

"You know Master would have to consent and settle on terms of payment." Anne stretched tall, relieving the tension of bending over the wash tub. The worry about America's future squeezed at her spine as well.

"I know." America straighten to her full height. "Papa, have you ever considered selling me? I probably could fetch a good price." She studied his face. Jeremiah was surprised at first, then panic washed down from his eyes to his slack jaw. He opened his mouth in protest when America interrupted. "I am happy to be here. I want to be hired out, though, so I can learn to read and be a proper maid." America was almost breathless with the last statement.

Anne responded in a pained voice. "Merry, you have no idea what you are getting into! There is no respect from whites who use slaves for their own needs."

"Papa does not use us that way," America stated. She spoke of him as he shook out the newspaper to study it. "He looks out for us. And he lined up work for you as a laundress. I think he will find work for me." Jeremiah listened, but chose not to respond.

Anne continued her story. "I am one of the fortunate ones. When Master bought me, I was so afraid he would just keep me as his fancy woman. He could take advantage of me like Master Henry because I was his property. I had been raped, ridiculed, and…reviled in Master Henry's house." There was a pause as she shook herself at the memory. "As you know, my life did not turn out the way it started. Most slave girls are not so lucky. You have seen them. And, you can tell by their skin color that they are property even before you see their faces."

America reasoned. "I am hoping for a chance to be free: a chance to rely on printed words. You have said that 'the truth will set you free.' Well, I think reading is a pathway to truth. I would use what you and Papa have set up and make it better-for all of us!" Sunshine broke through the grief on America's face. "Papa, when would I start work for the Morgans?"

"Merry, we must find out if the big house is the best for you–if Master and Mistress Morgan are safe for you. Otherwise, you could be in for a lot of abuse working there." Jeremiah sounded like the businessman and livery owner he was.

Anne pushed a stained wet dress down with such vigor that soapy water splashed on the floor around the tub. "You are looking to be a house girl just so you can learn to read?" She showed her exasperation. "And, who in that family is going to teach you?"

"Oh, I do not know. In that house, I would be surrounded by the comforts of fine furniture and books and gentle people." America glanced at the sturdy but heavily used wooden kitchen table and the durable secondhand chairs. "I looked in the windows one afternoon as I passed by. There are painted pictures in frames, books in glass-front cabinets, china figurines, newspapers on a very large desk."

"Surrounded. You say surrounded. Your time surrounded by all those niceties is not your own." Anne raised her voice. "You would be tending to the master or mistress or their children. And, you should know, slave owners are usually not gentle, in spite of their manners and clothes and social etiquette. They demand your complete obedience."

"Oh, Mama, you are speaking from your experience as a slave. I would be a hired servant. Papa would…"

Anne interrupted. "We are *slaves*. Never forget that." She looked straight at Jeremiah. "Master Murphy, please tell her. You hire me out to earn more money for you." She turned to America as if confiding a secret. "Master gets paid for the laundry work I do for his customers. But, Merry, thanks to him we have a place to call our home and the appearance of being free colored."

"Yes, Merry," Jeremiah cut in. "What your mama says is true. Because I own you and love you both, you are safe with me."

"We are like your horses." America's blunt statement challenged him.

Chapter 8
Contract

JEREMIAH TOOK A NOISY SIP OF THE SASSAFRAS TEA and solemnly looked at America, waiting for her to explain her last abrupt remark, comparing slaves to horses. America perched on one of the chairs at the large table, facing Jeremiah.

The unpretentious room served as the kitchen, living room, and laundry for the small, sturdy home. He had purchased the dwelling because it was not far from his livery stable. Anne liked it because she could count on the help and support from friends close by. With a few household goods from Moses Spencer's secondhand furniture store, Anne had made the house Jeremiah Murphy's home, a haven of love and comfort. America's presence had added joy and peace to the peculiar relationship of master and slave.

The daughter softened her attitude. "Papa, I think I could do a good job as a house girl and make you and Mama proud."

"Uncle Eli told me that Mistress Henrietta spoke of the advantages of *hiring* a slave as opposed to *buying* one. Yes. Hiring out suits my way of thinking. I do *not* want to sell you." Jeremiah wanted to be clear about his motives.

"So, Master Murphy," America had pressed her appeal, ignoring his words of reassurance. "Will you draw up the papers?"

"Not so fast. I plan to find work for you, but I don't yet know if the Morgan household is satisfactory, in spite of the wealth and good name."

"When will you know?"

"When I learn more about how you would fit in." As if to change the subject, Jeremiah leaned back in his chair near the fireplace, adjusted the oil lamp, and folded the newspaper to the advertisement columns. "Aah, my notice is in the paper. I hope travelers and traders see it."

"May I see it?" America squinted at the paper. Nothing on the printed page made sense to her except the drawings of horses, equipment, and runaway slave symbols. "What is your notice?"

"For my livery." He pointed to the small announcement at the bottom of the page. "Why do you want to know?"

"Oh, I do not want to know about your stable, but I do want to know how to read about it. That is why I am so interested in being hired out as a house girl."

"How is that?" Jeremiah folded the paper flat.

"Because," America repeated her opinion. "I figure that if I am in a fine house with books and paintings and papers, I will learn to read." She clasped her hands in a hopeful fist.

"It does not work that way." Murphy explained. "They will be looking to hire someone to work." He looked at America intently as if studying a horse. "If I think you are right for the job, I have to convince them that you are trustworthy, honest, and will quickly learn their rules. Master Morgan would decide if you are worth the money, and he would pay me for your work."

"You own me like you own the horses in your stable." America repeated the fact.

Jeremiah's quick look at Anne revealed her unsmiling but knowing gaze.

"Yes." He sighed.

Anne stopped mixing the cornbread dough. In an emotion-filled voice and with pleading eyes, she said, "Merry, you need to understand. Master wants what is good for you."

America pushed away from Anne's statement. It was easier to reject her mama's reasoning than her papa's. "Learning to read would be good for me."

Jeremiah explained. "That is not half of what I have to consider." He paused, putting down the newspaper. "Color is important. It can rule how a customer decides." He looked at his pink-tinged white hands, stained brown from stable chores. "People judge you by your looks. They look at your color first, guess at your age, and take notice of your clothes. All of that gives owners or traders an idea of what you can do before they show any interest."

"How the stock looks has to be considered before anything else? Papa, is that what you do? Make your property presentable so the customer will buy it or hire it? You take care of the stables and the carriages, give the horses good feed and water." America pointedly referred to ownership of a livery stable. "You make your horses respectable, just as you do for Mama and me." She paused to study the effect her words had on her parents. Even though her comparison to horses was mild, America revealed the sting to her pride. She, indeed, was somebody's property. She went on. "It doesn't matter what color a horse is."

"Actually, it does." Jeremiah wanted facts to serve as buffers to the emotions that were present but hidden. "Customers ask for matched pairs of gray trotters, or they want a chestnut palomino, or a black stallion. By demanding a specific color in business dealings, the patron feels a greater sense of control, which is a sign of wealth."

"Owners pick out a slave or horse by how they look and act." America used the information, thinking how it applied to herself and to slaves on the auction block. "If we appear suitable and do what an owner says, then he will take care of us." Her eyes confronted him.

"Yesss. Usually." Jeremiah Murphy hesitated because of his knowledge to the contrary, but he tried to be honest. *I know kind owners. Dash it, I'm one myself!*

"What if we do not want to do as you say?"

"Now, Merry, you know about that." Papa tried to be gentle. "We come to an understanding..."

"Usually slave owners do not take the time for understanding," Anne broke in. "They demand immediate obedience. And many do not take care of their slaves." Anne had raised her voice.

"Do you think Master Morgan would be like that?" America expressed the fear they all hid in their hearts.

"I have to find out. You would be hired out to Master Morgan and treated as one of his slaves."

"But, would I come home to you every day?" America understood the harm.

"I don't know." Jeremiah reflected Anne's apprehension and America's concern. "As I said before, color is important."

"Color. For house girls?"

"Yes. The color of your skin." Jeremiah nodded and smiled at the beauty of America's looks. "Most whites consider a slave with lighter skin to be smarter, easier to train."

"Well, I am smart and easy to train. You know how handy I am with Mama's work." America stated her confidence.

"Yes." Then he added, "You learn all of Anne's ways and I can hire you out as the best laundress in Lexington." A smile crossed his face.

"I want to be better than that! I want to read." America pointed at the newspaper, then turned it around to view the front page. She realized her parents had not grasped her ideas of reading and freedom. "Would you teach me to read, Papa?"

"Why?" Jeremiah's blunt question challenged her.

America's apron-covered figure became very still. "So, I can find out more than what people just tell me."

"Yes. You *can* get closer to the truth." He smiled. But his face sobered. "You are wondering if I would teach you. No."

America interrupted him, continuing her train of thought, to avoid listening to Jeremiah's excuses. "And, to show that a slave can learn whatever there is to learn."

"By becoming a house girl? Are you looking to prove that you could pass for white?"

"No, Papa. I will always be true to myself. I want a chance to understand the language of the printed word."

Jeremiah avoided making excuses for not teaching America. Her motives had just dawned on him. "Merry, you are willing to work toward getting your freedom by reading, in spite of the handicap of your color."

"Yes, Papa." America had reason to hope. Her Master Murphy would support her, although he would not teach her to read. She decided to make excuses for him: "I know you do not have time to teach me."

"Well, I am not trained to be a teacher. That should be left to spinsters and bookish fellows. But, I promise you: I will find out the requirements for a house girl at Hopemont." He enthusiastically thumped the paper on the table.

Hesitantly, Anne spoke up. "I will ready you on the duties of a house servant."

"Oh, Mama, I will make Papa ever so proud!"

⁂ ⁂ ⁂

A week later, Jeremiah came home with a folded document tucked inside his dark wool suit coat. After their usual greeting, he waited as America and Anne cleared the kitchen table of ironing materials by folding the freshly starched and ironed shirts and carefully stacking them in a large wicker basket. Anne set the water kettle to boil while he produced the one-page, handwritten contract. Smoothing it on the still warm table, he inspected it. "I looked into how you would fit in with the Morgan family, Merry. Uncle Eli thinks Master Calvin and Mistress Henrietta are all right. The mistress is looking for a house girl and companion for her niece Catherine." He cleared his throat and read the document aloud.

"On the 1st of September, 1854, I promise to pay to Jeremiah Murphy the sum of $60.00 for the hire of his girl America, as trained and directed by my servant Aunt Bette, for work as a housemaid during the coming 6 months. Jeremiah Murphy will provide shelter and clothing for his servant girl and pay taxes for her hire. Dated this March 1, 1854." Jeremiah paused. "Then there is space for Master Morgan to sign."

America chirped and clapped her hands. "Papa, is my name really on that paper?" When she saw his nod, she demanded, "Where is it?"

"Right here, America." Jeremiah pointed. "See the rounded letter that is bigger? That's an A for America."

"Oh, Papa. That is my first reading lesson!"

Anne bowed her head.

"Mama, this is my chance," America paused, "for a good life."

"Merry, you must do the best with what you have."
Her mama sighed at the change that was coming.

"Yes, Mama. You will see."

"Now, Aunt Bette will be a help," Jeremiah explained.
"The Morgans call her 'Aunt' because she has been with
the family so long. I put that condition in the contract,
along with the clothing, shelter, and taxes that I provide.
That should justify my ownership rights and secure
Merry's living quarters. The owners put great store in
Aunt Bette's ability. She will be your safety, so you do as
she directs, Merry."

"Yes, Papa. I will learn from her."

Chapter 9
Schooling

IN TWO MONTHS, AMERICA HAD LEARNED the daily routine of life at Hopemont from Aunt Bette. Since her kidnapping just weeks ago, she realized she had a reliable ally in Cook. Even Catherine appeared to encourage her reading interest.

"America, put these Walter Scott books in the basket with the other reading things." Catherine stood on a stool in Calvin Morgan's office library, surveying the shelves of the tall, well-organized bookcase. "They have good stories to share. I want to read some aloud to you, especially the poems." Even though Catherine was younger, her authority over America was taken for granted.

"I don't know if the basket is big enough to hold everything."

"Take out the ink pot and rags and the quills. I'll keep them in my room after all. We won't be practicing penmanship." Catherine noticed that Aunt Bette had stepped inside the room. She ignored the adult servant but made sure she heard her next words. "And, my embroidery pieces are still up there too. After you've learned the letters, then we can work on the samplers." She purposefully mentioned the needlework chores as the reason for the reading lessons.

"Now, Miss Catherine, those letters on the samplers would be easy for America to copy without learning them. Lord knows she is handy with the needle." Aunt Bette nodded to America as she talked with Catherine. "But it is up to you to do them. America can teach you all the stitches you need, but we can't have her wasting time learning the letters and words. There is too much work to be done in this house. If you want to while away your time reading to your maid servant, you will need to get permission from Miss Henrietta."

Catherine was surprised to hear Aunt Bette seemingly thwart her plans. Her face showed her confusion and dismay. America looked down at her hands, as a feeling of betrayal swept over her.

After a few moments to collect herself, Catherine addressed Aunt Bette. "Neither my time nor hers, for that matter, would be wasted by teaching America to read. She is smart enough to learn quickly and use the knowledge for the benefit of this household. She could read stories for the grandchildren in the nursery. She could run errands, deliver notes, and purchase items that relied on the written word. She could find Bible passages to read to fellow servants." Catherine tapped her foot to emphasize her statements. "There are many blacks who *do* know how to read in this city. Someone must…"

Aunt Bette raised the palm of her hand to stop Catherine's discourse. "Now, Miss Catherine. I can see how you want to share stories and reading with America. You have set out on that course by using the sampler as the reason to work with letters and words. That seems as good as any I have heard."

"Then why are you thinking up reasons to go against my plan?" Catherine placed her hand on her hip.

"Mistress Henrietta will see right through it." Aunt Bette knew a thing or two about diplomacy. She wanted to prepare Catherine to justify to her aunt the anticipated reading lessons. "Exactly why have you chosen your servant girl to read with?"

"America always looks on the bright side. She's well-mannered without being prim. She is quick to learn anything you show her. And, I would like to see what she thinks of stories about other people and places." America separated herself by standing off to one side, but she listened closely.

Aunt Bette's voice was firm. "Here's another reason to add when you talk to Mistress Henrietta. Remind her that in Kentucky, blacks have been taught. It's not against the law. In the states south of here, the whites are afraid of educating blacks-so they have laws forbidding it. But not here." The senior servant showed her support of Catherine's plan.

The next day, Catherine and Mistress Henrietta reached an understanding. The reading lessons would commence in the afternoons when America fulfilled her duties as house servant. A scheme developed. When the noon meal was completed and the dining room put in order, Catherine came to the pantry and read aloud to America and Cook as they worked on supper preparations and meal chores. At Catherine's signal, America would then sit at the small table under the window for her lessons.

America excitedly pulled out the items in the basket. "This slate, Miss Catherine. You took it back and forth to your school. Does it help with reading?"

"Yeesss," Catherine gave a sly grin. "That's why it is among the other things..."

"How does it help you read?" America turned it over, noticing the white powder in the corners of the frame.

"It is like the small blackboard that the teacher uses in the classroom."

"Blackboard," America echoed. "It is black. Do you scratch on it with one of those white pieces of limestone?"

"Write," corrected Catherine. "The teacher *writes* words on it with the limestone chalk for us to read. That's what I plan to do."

"Then you clean it off?"

"Yes," Catherine nodded and held up her slate. "You can have that task, as I'm sure you would be better at it than I would. The white pieces crumble and turn into powder and get all over my apron and into the frame. I keep losing the lump of limestone, too."

"Huh. You read white words on a writing board that is black. But words in books are black printed on white paper."

"America, the *color* of letters is not important."

"Oh, so letters are letters," America understood immediately. "Like people are people."

Catherine nodded. "When you get to know the letters, then you'll learn the words-and be reading! I will show you the letters and we can put them together to read."

"Then I can read anything I want, Miss Catherine." America giggled. "That!" She pointed to the receipt book Mistress Henrietta kept to read to Cook or Aunt Bette. "And that!" She picked up a folded newspaper left on the mantel. "And that!" She handed Catherine one of the Walter Scott books.

"We can start tomorrow," Catherine said, excited. "I'll find a good lump of limestone for writing, since I'm to be the teacher."

"And, I will find a surprise for you." America thought of a small item for Catherine's slate.

The next day, America surprised Catherine with her recognition of the letters *A*, *E*, and *C*. Jeremiah had shown her those letters in print form, as part of her name. Catherine quickly acquainted her with *B*, *D*, and *F*. The girls sat close together, the servant maid's braided dark hair a quiet contrast to the auburn locks of her mistress's bouncing ringlets. America took her learning very seriously. But Catherine viewed playing school as a comfortable frolic in literature with a kind, thoughtful companion.

By the time the week was over, Catherine had introduced America to all the letters and the sounds as they studied her primary reader. America had memorized the order of the alphabet and Catherine taught her an alphabet song.

"Miss Catherine, I have a surprise for you." America pulled two white fabric pieces out of the basket.

Folded and hemmed, the items looked like small napkins, which confused her young mistress. "For my hope chest?"

"Look at the corner of each square," directed America.

"America, what are these? Oh, there's a shape of a cat on each one! Cat?" She did not understand as she inspected the objects.

"Cat." America replied, pointing to her embroidery handiwork. "The cat shape shows they belong to you, Miss Catherine. The squares are to wipe the chalk dust from your slate."

"Ahh, how clever! You are so handy, although I expect you to use the squares more than I will. Is there a reason you made two?" Catherine wanted to know details.

"Yes, Miss Catherine. One to use and one for extra."

"A spare square," her young mistress murmured with a wink.

"Yes. I will use a square with care to wipe the slate bare." America smiled.

America reviewed what she had learned about the letters of the alphabet. "And this is G. It looks like C except it has an arm turned in." America looked at Catherine for confirmation, tucking her right arm across her middle as she raised her left arm in an arc over her head. So fascinated with learning that she was oblivious to Aunt Bette's raised eyebrows.

54

Catherine nodded. After looking over to see if Cook was watching too, she asked, "America, what's next?"

"Let me see. *H*, I think." America moved her head from side to side in rhythm to the rhyme in her head. "Yes. But there's something I need to remember about the *G*: it can sound like another letter."

"*J*," said Catherine. "Don't worry about that. Let's just get to know all the letters now."

"Miss Catherine, I want to know..."

"I never should have brought it up when I did." Catherine frowned and looked out the pantry window, then turned to explain. "A word that begins with *G*-like gossip-or goodbye-sounds like it came from your throat. But some *G* words are softer and seem to come from your mouth-like genuine-or gingerbread and it sounds more like a *J*."

"Why?"

Catherine sighed. *Oh, how does Mistress Dunham have the patience to teach?*

America gave her a knowing look. "Miss Catherine, I know this is tiresome for you because you know these letters backwards and forward. I want to know them as well as you-all twenty-six of them. I want to be friends with the letters."

Catherine couldn't help but smile. "You have to learn them first, America, to get to 'Reading Land.'"

"Reading Land?" America frowned. "What do you mean? There is no..." She grinned. "You are playing with me. All right. The next after *H* is *I*. Eye?" She pointed to her eye.

"No," laughed Catherine. "That's spelled with an *E*." The look on America's face led Catherine to say, "Please, just take my word for it."

"Does *I* mean me?" America was cautious. "*I* think *I* know that you will say yes."

"Yes, America. Keep going."

Chapter 10
Respect

"THE NEXT LETTER IS J, AND THEN K, L, AND M," America said in a rush. "*M* for Master and Mistress and Miss." America gave a small bow and curtsy. *I must show respect even though I do not actually feel it.*

"America, why do you persist calling me Miss Catherine? We are friends. Why do you have to be so formal?" Catherine realized that when she returned to live with Aunt Mary and Uncle John in Frankfort, she would be served by her cringing Hattie again.

"You are white and I am colored," America said. "Master Murphy told me I need to watch how I appear to others."

"By being so proper?" Catherine was confused. "You seem to have perfect manners when you are around white people."

"Many, many people think we are stupid, slothful savages." America paused. Her frown turned to a smile. "Ah, Ha! *Ssstupid, ssslothful sssavages.* "Those words all begin with the same sound. An *S*?"

"Yes." Catherine added. "And, I know you are *not* a stupid savage."

"And, I do not have time to be slothful if I am to learn how to read."

56

"Why is reading so important to you?" Catherine asked. The simple wooden chair at the little table was uncomfortable. She felt out of place in the servants' work room. The pantry was America's and Cook's domain even though her wishes were always attended to. When she rose to stretch and loosen her twisted linen petticoat, America stood up to clear off the table, as well as show her manners as a servant.

"Well, I would like to know how life is as a free person," America said as she packed the fabric square and primary reader back in the basket.

"Your papa is free, isn't he? He's white." Catherine stated the obvious.

"I am his slave. I am lucky that Master Murphy is good to me, but I am his property as well as his daughter. Sometimes I feel as if I am a loveable buckskin workhorse." America shrugged her shoulders, knowing that she had spoken too freely.

"Well, what do you want?" Catherine showed her impatience. She and JW were orphans. Although her Aunt Mary and Uncle John were their guardians, she still felt abandoned-and unloved-now that her parents were gone.

"I want to be free. I want people to judge me as a person, not as an animal who must do the bidding of the master." America frowned in thought and picked her words carefully. "I cannot speak for myself or do anything I want, like a white girl can."

"America, I can't do anything I want," Catherine said, laughing derisively. "I'm not allowed to climb trees or stay out after dark. I have to go to the Female Academy, and you know that I must make those wearisome samplers."

"You do not have to guard against slave catchers!" America's words sizzled like large drops of rain on a hot pavement.

Catherine was surprised. She had never heard America so frustrated. Aunt Bette heard the exchange and strode over, opening her mouth for a scolding. When she saw the perplexed look on America's face, she dropped her hand and shook her head.

"America, I," Catherine paused. She didn't know what to say. *America had been kidnapped by that slave stealer only a month ago! She is right. My life is easier because I am white — and free.*

America stamped her foot and turned away from Catherine. After a moment, she turned back to face her. "Miss Catherine, Master Murphy has reminded us more than once that we must follow the slave codes. I know we have to work at it. Mama and I have to show a piece of paper to anyone we work for that says we are registered to Jeremiah Murphy. He showed me my name written on it. Since I cannot read, I do not know exactly what it says. It is aggravating."

Catherine could almost understand America's exasperation. When she was younger and didn't know how to read, she carried around a Mother Goose book, hoping it would help her decipher the words in it.

"What I would *like* to do is learn to read." America voiced her uneasiness.

Catherine didn't say anything.

"And, there are more foolish rules," America continued. "Anytime Mama tries to buy something from white folk, she has to show her certificate of permission. When Master Murphy hires us out for work, the first thing the patron asks for is his proof of ownership."

Catherine was astonished. Her wide-eyed look toward Cook was met with a sad, soulful acknowledgment. The young mistress's thoughts, like the cream that Cook was processing in the blue stoneware butter churn, were whirling around and resting on nothing of substance. *No one in her family has to prove their status. A piece of paper makes all the difference. Color decides: white is free, black is not.*

58

"It is almost like I am a horse," America murmured, intending to demonstrate that slaves were treated as livestock. "No. Of course not. But you do have the same skin color as some I've seen." Catherine teased, trying to lighten the conversation.

America huffed and folded her arms across her chest.

"I didn't make those foolish rules," Catherine said petulantly. "I don't see why you are angry at me."

"White people run things and make the rules."

"*I* don't run things. But there must be a reason," replied Catherine. "Come to think. In a way it protects you. If someone accuses you of being an escaped slave and gets ready to haul you away, you can show them your papers!"

"Do you really think a slave catcher would stop me and ask," America put her hand on one hip as she impersonated a bounty hunter, "now, are you a runaway or not?"

Catherine did not know what to say: she didn't have to prove anything. She also realized that she was torn between laughing at America's acting and crying at her circumstances.

"Oh, let us get back to the letters," said America. "After *L* is *M*."

"*M* is for Miss Catherine," the young mistress interrupted. "I still want to know why you insist on addressing me as Miss Catherine. My family just calls me Catherine, which begins…" She sat down and motioned to America to finish the sentence.

"With a *C*," America obliged.

"You are like family to me, America." Catherine almost whined as she remembered the planned move back to Frankfort. "Why do you have to be so formal?"

America stared at her. "Miss Catherine, it is to show respect. Master Murphy said we need to be as polite as we can to people who could help us. Showing respect is our way to point out that we are worth the trouble. You call your teacher Miss Dunham out of respect. Well, I call my teacher, Miss Catherine."

"Miss Dunham is older and wiser, and I call her by her proper name because I'd be in trouble if I didn't."

"It is the same thing. You are older and wiser in reading and writing, and I would be in trouble if I did not call you Miss Catherine." America sat down at the small table again because Catherine had. "Let me see. The next letters are N, O, P, Q, R. Do you spell 'are' with just that one letter like I?"

"No. 'Are' is spelled beginning with an A. Don't try to get all the rules in your head at once."

"I want to learn as much…"

"As I know," Catherine finished her sentence. "It takes time, though. Huh. I'm a poet and don't know it. Reading Land is full of poets, I promise.

Chapter 11
Manners

THE NEXT DAY AMERICA WAS POLISHING THE SLATE with one of her handmade wiping cloths when Catherine entered the pantry. "Miss Catherine," America addressed her, standing. "Maybe you could show me how to draw the letters on the slate."

"You *write* letters, you don't *draw* them, or *scratch* them," Catherine reminded her. "But, I have a better idea. It is so hot in here today. We can sit on the porch upstairs and catch a breeze. The chairs are bigger and easy. I can show you the words in the book as I read to you."

The explanation was to inform Aunt Bette and Cook of her plans as well as to tell America what she had in mind. They did not try to stop her. Catherine pulled from the basket her primary reader and a poetry book. She handed them to America. The girls climbed the back stairs to the second-floor area and the porch, which offered shelter and distance from the main part of the house.

"This is *Lullaby of an Infant Chief*." Catherine opened the book to a Walter Scott poem. "It is one of my favorites. I will read just the first stanza to see if you like it, too: "O hush thee, my baby, thy sire was a knight, Thy mother a lady, both lovely and bright; /The woods and the glens, from the towers which we see, /They all are belonging, dear baby, to thee." She read Walter Scott's words in a lilting voice that reflected the rhyming pattern.

"Oh, Miss Catherine." America clasped her hands. "It is lovely. I hope to remember it and surprise Master Murphy when I am ready. Could you read it again so I can get it in my head?"

"I will. I'm glad you like it. We must work on it every day until you can say it from memory, and then I will teach you the other two stanzas."

"Yes. Thank you. Now, shall I go get the slate and chalk for my lesson?" America remembered the reason for sitting with her young mistress.

"No. Let's play I Spy," instructed Catherine, tired of playing school for the past ten days. "I look around and say, 'I spy with my little eye something brown'. You look around and name all the brown things you see. When you guess the right one, then it's your turn to spy something and I have to guess."

"All right, Miss Catherine," America said without much enthusiasm.

"I spy with my little eye something green."

"Your dress. Table." America glanced at Catherine who was looking across the porch. "Leaves!"

"Yes." Catherine clapped her hands, delighted. "Now it is your turn."

"I spy with my..." America stopped. "Oh, Miss Catherine!" She looked bewildered.

"Now, America. You are to tell me the color of what you see."

"Miss Catherine, I see a..." America paused, and then remembered the words, "I spy with my little eye a white man. Look over there." America motioned the direction with a nod of her head.

"You aren't allowed to give any hints." Catherine was disappointed that America was not playing the game properly; however, she did look in the direction America indicated.

"Who is he? What is he doing?" America had forgotten the game they were playing.

Catherine shrugged. "Well, he is looking at this house. I think he is trying to find a good perspective. See his sketchbook? And the graphite stick?"

"Yes, I see now. He is making drawings." America breathed easier. "He must be an artist-but a poor one at that. He isn't dressed very well."

"Maybe he is an architect, hired to make the Bruce house match the looks of this place, so he needs a rendering to study." Catherine's imagination was as busy as the lines on the sketchpad. "You know Cousin Johnny lives there. He moved across the street when he married Miss Becky Bruce a few years ago. That house is not nearly as grand as this." Catherine shrugged again. "See how short that man is? His size is like the size of that house compared to Hopemont."

America relaxed. The man's height and clothes did not match the tall, handsomely attired look of her kidnapper. Having folded his sketchbook, pocketed his piece of graphite, and adjusted his hat, he strolled down Mill Street. "He startled me, standing there so still and quiet," she explained. "But I guess he would have to concentrate on drawing what he *sees*."

"I'm surprised that you even noticed him." Catherine put a marker in her Walter Scott book and laid it on the table. "I've seen many people in that cleared area in front of this house. They should make it a public garden. Let's play I Spy."

"All right. I spy with my little eye something black," said America, relief showing in her face.

Catherine, a veteran of the game, studied the direction of America's gaze. "Tree. Light post. Iron fence! It's the fence, isn't it?"

"Yes, Miss Catherine. You are good at this. But could we finish the alphabet? We got as far as *R* yesterday. There are not that many more letters."

A compromise came to mind. Catherine said, "I spy with my little eye something that starts with the next letter of the alphabet."

Immediately interested, America straightened up and her eyes twinkled. "Let me see. *P, Q, R*. We stopped at *R*. So, it is *S*. Something that starts with *S. Ssssssss.*" America looked in the direction of Catherine's gaze, which was down. "Sampler. Stick. Schoolbook!"

"Yes."

"Oh, Miss Catherine, it will be fun playing I Spy with words. I will be able to learn so much more about them that way."

"You will need to know what the words look like. We can work with this lesson book tomorrow."

America could not hold back her excitement. "Oh, Miss Catherine. You are such a good teacher. Mama is especially glad that I am here with you."

"Why?" Catherine asked.

"She now sees the advantages of me working here."

Catherine studied America, suddenly suspicious. "That is why she's glad I am your mistress?"

A confused look crossed America's face. "And, because learning from you is so much fun."

"Well, playing school should be fun for both of us," said Catherine, with somewhat of an edge to her voice. "What does your master think? About reading?"

"Oh, Master Murphy is pleased, too." America fanned herself with her hands, more to relieve tension than to cool herself. "He wants to show people that I can learn and get ahead."

Catherine pulled her damp bodice away from her back. "So, I'm going to be your ticket to freedom?" *Is this why America is being so friendly with me?*

64

"Yessss." America's smile vanished. "Oh, no!" she said and clapped her hands to her face as if she had made a big mistake. "Miss Catherine, I did not mean it that way," America replied quickly. "Master Murphy wants to make things better for us. He can read but does not have the time or knowledge to teach me. He thinks that learning how to read and showing respect to people who could help me is how I can help myself."

"What do *you* think, America?" Catherine asked. "Do you think that is the best thing to do-to make things better for yourself? I sometimes pretend I don't like going to school, which Aunt Mary and Uncle John think is the best thing for me. **I** want to decide what to do." She placed her hand on her chest as if to emphasize her words. "Pure willfulness."

America looked at her as if she had grown a big wart on her nose. "I would give anything to be able to go to school and read." *Color decides.*

Catherine was embarrassed. "Well, I can be too outspoken. I really do like the lessons and the stories. The academy is my Reading Land, along with Uncle Calvin's library. I just don't want Aunt Henrietta and Aunt Mary to think they can direct my whole life. Or JW's life."

"I have to do what my parents tell me," America said. "There is really no choice if I want a better life. To know what white folk know would be useful," she said. "I feel foolish and left out because I cannot read-beside all the other things I cannot do."

"Yes." Catherine did not elaborate. She would not support anything that would jeopardize her own status or convenience.

"Miss Catherine." America looked down at her hands. "Have you ever been around someone who knows a secret but will not tell you?"

"Of course. There are some girls who act so high and mighty at Miss Dunham's academy. I think they are mean."

"Well, that is how I feel when I see someone reading," America admitted. "It is like they are keeping a secret, and I cannot ever figure it out."

"Speaking of secrets, America, I feel that you are keeping a secret from me." Catherine nodded and tapped her toe. She hesitated, then blurted out: "Did your master hire you out to Aunt Henrietta so you could learn to pass for white?"

America looked surprised. Then, she said, "No." But she did not offer an explanation.

Catherine waited. When America didn't say anything else, Catherine said, "I want to be like a friend, America. A teacher friend."

"Oh, Miss Catherine," America replied. "You have so much that I want. You go to school, and you have books and new clothes." She stopped and swallowed.

"Are you jealous?" cried Catherine. "I hope not. That would be the ruination of a friendship."

"No, Miss Catherine, I am not jealous." America was emphatic. "Mama has told me that we have to work with what we have in life. I was born a slave and you were born free. We each must make the best of our circumstances." She paused. "I want to learn," she stopped herself again, "how to be first-rate, to prove that people my color are just as good as white people."

"Well, America, I don't know if you are as good as me, but you certainly are as smart." Catherine gave her a sly sideways smile. "Now, I spy with my little eye something that starts with T."

"Tan?" America's mind was still on skin color. As a person of mixed race, she was usually described as *yellow* or *bright*, but she had heard *tan* used to explain her skin color, too. However, Catherine shook her head at America's guess, so she tried again. "Twig? Toe?"

"It can be what you call someone." Catherine's hint confused America.

"Their name? That does not-" America hesitated, trying to think of a name that started with *T*.

"No. Here is another hint. It's what you call the name of a book."

"Any book? Each one has a different name, like people!" America had the same sinking feeling that Catherine, like all people who could read, had a secret she was keeping from her.

"What do you call me?" Catherine demanded.

"Miss Catherine!" the two girls said her name together, giggling at the harmonious sound they made.

"*Miss* is my *title*, America." Catherine looked somewhat smug. "*Title* is also what you call any book's name."

"Yes, Miss Catherine." Disheartened that she had not figured out Catherine's hints, America became quiet, slipping back to her submissive role.

Catherine, wanting to keep the budding friendship on solid ground, tried to lighten the conversation. "Well, if you persist in calling me by my title, I will just have to make up a title for you. How about Amazing America, or Good Girl, or…"

"America will do," she softly interrupted, looking at her hands. A light wind changed the temperature, along with the mood of the game. *Am I shivering from the cool breeze? Or embarrassment?*

"Tomorrow we will play I Spy again, America," Catherine said.

"Miss Catherine, I would be honored to do that. Thank you for your time. I really like the Walter Scott poem you have shared with me." America's reply was rather stiff and was followed by a small bow.

Once again, she was showing her best manners.

Chapter 12
Tucky

THE GIRLS BEGAN TO USE THE SECOND-FLOOR PORCH as their schoolroom. The hot summer days offered little relief for the urgency to deal with reading and needlework quests. Besides the Walter Scott lullaby poem they practiced every day, Catherine read passages from her primary reader, pointing to the words as America listened. Then they would go through the accompanying spelling word list. An enthusiastic student, America absorbed two reading lessons at a time.

Catherine, a wayward pupil on the subject of embroidery, was easily distracted from working on the sampler. Aunt Bette saw to it that the embroidery hoop, scissors, needles, and floss were close by, but she did not urge her young mistress to work with them. Very often a completed design on the sampler would lead Catherine to visit Reading Land and, of course, take America along, indulging in a story from a favorite book.

One warm sunny morning, Aunt Mary and Uncle John arrived in their horse-drawn barouche. They took Catherine and JW out to Grandfather Hunt's farm on Leestown Pike. Catherine had not been to the farm since the months after their mother died. She looked at it with a new understanding of the necessary labor involved. A few slaves were weeding the young hemp plants that would soon grow into tall sturdy stalks. Others were clearing fields for planting, and still others were tending livestock. The workers looked rough. Both men and women wore misshapen, broad-brimmed hats whose sole purpose was to protect the wearer from the sun's hot rays. Their ill-fitting clothes shielded them from the harsh plants and gritty dirt. *They look sad and uneasy. These people could be America's relatives.*

Grateful to consider animals rather than slaves, Catherine asked JW if he remembered any of Grandfather Hunt's horses.

"Yes. I remember those twin chestnut foals. They were searching for their mama just like we were." JW frowned at the memory. "And, I remember a racehorse they named Frank Forester. Its name is the pen name of a famous writer in New York."

"I wonder if the writer could write as fast as the runner could run?"

"Only if Forester the writer could write a mile of words in two and a half minutes." JW strolled over to investigate the horses in their paddocks, offering bits of carrots he had stashed in his pockets.

Aunt Mary and Catherine walked around the grounds and pasture areas as Uncle John talked with the farm manager, Mr. Marrs. The overseer directed a house slave to bring out a litter of puppies in a basket for Catherine to see. As working dogs, the black and white pups would soon be herding livestock. *Grandfather Hunt bought the dogs to work, just as he bought slaves. The blacks aren't any better off than the dogs. I'll look at the puppies to be polite. That's what America would do.*

The six puppies tumbled out of the basket and began investigating. The smallest pup found Catherine. She first nuzzled her hand and then licked it from finger to wrist.

That did it: Catherine was hooked. She sat down in the grass of the front lawn and the puppy climbed into her lap. "That little one is what I call the runt of the litter," said Mister Marrs. "I didn't think the female would care for it like the others. But, that young pup pushed her weight around to get noticed, and it worked."

"She is so friendly! Do you have a name for her?" Catherine asked.

"No. We won't be keeping her. Because of her size, she would not be serviceable for herding livestock." Mister Marrs paused and then quickly addressed her, "Would you like to keep the pup? She has been weaned, so you should be able to handle her with no trouble."

"Oh, yes, Mister Marrs! With Aunt Mary and Uncle John's permission, of course." Catherine glanced at them. Uncle John gave a slight nod, and she looked back down at the puppy. *My own pet! And she is just right!*

On the way home, Catherine considered a name for her black-and-white dog. "I want the name to be special but show that she is from around here. JW, can you help me?"

"How about Hunt Dog?" JW offered. "She's a dog and belongs to the Hunts."

"I don't like that. What about La Fayette?" Catherine thought aloud.

"Sounds too much like the marquis, General Lafayette. Huh. I just can't think of a good name for your dog." JW turned in his seat and watched the movement of the horses pulling the barouche. "Grandfather could certainly pick good thoroughbreds and Standardbreds, but he wasn't so good with names. Me neither." JW then straightened himself and addressed his aunt and uncle. "Do you think Uncle Tom will bring me out here to see the horses?"

"I don't see why he wouldn't. He loves horses and likes to see about their care and well-being." Uncle John gave good advice.

"Tucky!" The name popped into Catherine's head. "That will be her name! Short for Kentucky. I can't wait to show her to America!"

Upon her return to Hopemont, Catherine arranged a wooden box for Tucky on the side porch next to the servants' door. Since America had departed for the day, the surprise introduction would have to wait until tomorrow. Meanwhile, Cook agreed to save scraps and bones for Tucky's meals, and Aunt Bette promised she would treat the dog as a new member of the family. Aunt Henrietta and Aunt Mary had a quick conference in the house office. When they appeared at the side door, it was Aunt Henrietta who spoke. "You know that she will be with you most of the time. You'll be in charge of feeding her and training her. It's a big responsibility."

Late in the evening, Catherine crept down to the porch to check on her pet nestled in the box.

"Catherine, you can't keep going outside. Tucky will be all right." It was the third time Mistress Henrietta noticed her niece at the side door near the pantry.

"Well, she has never been away from the rest of her pack. She must be lonely." Catherine gazed into Tucky's coffee-brown eyes. Tucky looked back, as if memorizing Catherine's face.

"I'm glad we didn't put her in the shed," Catherine said. "This box is more comfortable and since it's next to the door, she can hear us when we come down in the morning."

"Oh, so you *do* plan to go to bed tonight!" her aunt teased. "Dawn will come before you know it, and Tucky will be here, ready for another adventure."

"All right, Aunt Henrietta." Catherine paused. "Do you think she will need another cover in the middle of the night?" she asked, leaning down to pet Tucky. The puppy was snuggled in her box. Her thick fur felt soft against Catherine's hand.

"No, Catherine." Then her aunt gave a lopsided grin. "And you *do* know: let sleeping dogs lie."

Early the next morning Catherine led Tucky around the yard inside the iron fence, before breakfast. The dog followed her, occasionally sniffing at the fence in a dog-like inspection of the perimeter. She seemed to understand that it was her territory to guard and protect. When Catherine walked outside the fence, Tucky hesitated and whined at the back gate.

"Good dog! You know how far you can go. We will get along wonderfully!"

When America arrived, Catherine could tell that neither companion was pleased to meet the other. Tucky, viewing America as a threat to guard against, began a slow growl and bared her teeth. When Catherine called her name in a commanding voice, Tucky stopped growling but remained watchful.

Ever mindful of her manners, America asked, "Does she bite? Will she chase me?"

"Oh, America, she's just a baby-only about three-months old. She hasn't learned to be mean." Catherine had not expected America to be afraid.

"Miss Catherine, I have heard that dogs can be cruel and vicious," America cautioned. "Slave owners have used dogs to attack or track down slaves."

"That's not going to happen with Tucky," Catherine said. "You'll see. She minds me."

"I will take you at your word. If Tucky is your companion, I should feel safe," America paused. "If I see her without you, though, I might go the other way."

Every morning when America arrived, Catherine would have Tucky close by to see their friendly greeting. That way, the dog understood that America was no threat.

Catherine had moved Tucky's box and bedding up to the second-floor porch, away from the temptation of food preparation in the pantry.

America brought scraps of butter or small bits of fat for Catherine's pet. The food offerings sealed the bargain of friendship. Eventually, Tucky's wagging tail showed she had accepted America as a friend.

Revealing the habits of her breed, Tucky entertained the girls more than once. As Catherine and America cooled themselves in the shade of the elm tree beyond the side porch, Tucky demonstrated the finer points of herding animals. Unfortunately, the animals she chose to herd were squirrels searching for food in the yard of Hopemont house. Tucky tried staring at them to reverse their forward movement. That method worked well. The squirrels ran in the opposite direction, just not where she intended them to go. Tucky tried to nip at their feet, but the wily squirrels were too fast. They ended the chase by charging up a sycamore tree. At the end of those encounters, Tucky returned to the company of the girls in a subdued manner-almost shaking her head as if wondering why the squirrels did not mind her. The squirrels added to the insult by chattering from the safety of the tree.

"Catherine, your Uncle John and I are going to take JW for an afternoon at the racetrack. Would you like to come along?" Just a week after Tucky arrived, Aunt Mary and Uncle John returned to Lexington on a shopping trip for the newly built Capital Hotel in Frankfort. When the business chore was finished, they called at Hopemont to visit with the Morgans and Catherine and JW.

"Aunt Mary, I'd like very much to see the horses race. May I take America with me?"

"She would be a help."

Uncle John and Aunt Mary sat in the forward-facing seats of the barouche while JW and Catherine viewed the passing neighborhoods of Lexington from the opposite perspective. America sat with the driver, a suitable perch for a house slave. The stately ornamental iron gates of the Kentucky Association Racecourse were open to allow the entry of patrons in carriages.

"Uncle John, the boys were talking about one of Doctor Warfield's horses winning his first race here last year as a three-year old. Four days later, he won the Citizens Stakes. But Doctor Warfield doesn't own him anymore. What happened?"

America turned to listen. She, too, heard Papa and Uncle Eli talking about this outstanding racehorse that was taken by his new owners to race in New Orleans. *Huh. The horse was sold down the river.*

"Well, JW, Doctor Warfield bred the horse and named it Darley. But, for racing, it was rented out to Harry Brown, a Negro. Harry was not allowed to race Darley in his name, even though he had leased and trained it. Blacks do not own racehorses." Uncle John was warming to the story.

Aunt Mary interrupted, "I remember Doctor Warfield when I was growing up at Hopemont. He and his family lived just down the street. My, he must be old by now!"

"Yes, Dear. I have heard that since he was getting too old to manage the horse himself, he sold it to Richard Ten Broeck, unbeknownst to Harry Brown." Uncle John showed his patience. "Harry lost all rights to the horse when Ten Broeck named a new trainer."

America shook her head. *If Harry knew how to read, things might have turned out differently.*

"Ten Broeck changed the name of the horse from Darley to-" Uncle John tapped his forehead, but had a slight, mischievous smile. "Oh, what is the new name?

75

Anyhow, he won his most recent race in New Orleans a month ago."

"Oh, oh, I know!" JW called out. "Cousin Johnny mentioned the name-a place name!"

"Lexington!" Catherine and JW sang out.

"Now, why couldn't I think of that?" Uncle John grinned slyly and then started humming. "Doo-dah. Doo-dah." The actual notes of the popular song stuck in everyone's mind. By the time they got back to Hopemont, young and not so young passengers were singing the Stephen Foster song: "The Camp town ladies sing this song/Doo-dah, Doo-dah/The Camp town racetrack's five miles long/Oh, de doo-dah day/Goin' to run all night/Goin' to run all day/I bet my money on a bob-tailed nag/Somebody bet on the gray."

Chapter 13
Plans

AMERICA SQUINTED AT THE BRIGHTNESS of the morning sun as she hurried along Upper Street on her way to Hopemont. She wished to speed up her duties as house servant that day so Miss Catherine's reading instructions could begin. Time was an enemy. Summer would be long gone just like the departure of a pesky mosquito when a swatter comes to hand. Catherine and JW would be leaving for Frankfort to live with Mary and John Hanna again, and America had not made friends with the printed word-yet.

She stopped on the boardwalk in front of Mister Bowyer's tailor shop. Was someone calling to her? The voice sounded oddly familiar. *Who could be wanting to get my attention?*

"Good morning, America!"

She saw him. And raised her hand in greeting. And smiled. And walked to the edge of the boardwalk. "Good morning to you, Jerry."

Master Skillman's handsome young servant raised his worn straw hat in greeting. He was driving a delivery wagon pulled by a muscular, well-nourished cart horse. The wagon rolled into the intersection of Upper and Main Street then it came to a sudden standstill. The force of the unexpected stop sent Jerry from his seat. He quickly regained his balance and control of the reins. He turned to look at the back wheels which were stuck in the mud of the unpaved portion of Upper Street. Climbing down from the driver's perch, Jerry made his way through the slop to the back of the wagon. He heaved one wheel upward. The power of his exertion and the straining of the horse against its harness was enough to roll the vehicle free of the gummy mire, splashing sludge as it rolled onto the solid macadam pavement. Once free of the oozing slop, the horse paused, resting against the harness traces. America thought their teamwork was perfect and wondered how many times they had worked together like that.

The rain that had come two days ago was a welcome ally, cutting the oppressive heat. But it had turned the streets into a soft yielding paste, binding fully laden vehicles to the clay-based mire.

"Heavy load, heavy mud!" Jerry had a lopsided smile, pleased that America had witnessed his physical and practical abilities. "How are you getting along with your reading lessons? I have seen you on the porch with Miss Catherine."

"Well enough, Jerry." America stepped closer to the wagon, minding her steps to avoid the sticky mud. She lowered her voice. "I hope to be reading by the time Miss Catherine leaves for Frankfort this fall."

"You will do fine. But, if you need any help, just let me know!" Jerry lowered his voice and looked around. "Master Skillman taught me when he saw I could help him. I made him proud."

America was excited at the prospect, and she was flattered that Jerry showed interest. But she knew manners required restraint. "Thank you, Jerry. I must be on my way this morning. I hope to see you again soon." She turned to continue her way on Upper Street as Jerry started down Main Street to deliver goods to the new bookstore.

Later that day, Henrietta handed Catherine her beginning sampler. "It must be completed by the end of summer. You brought it unfinished when you arrived here. I will not have you taking that sampler back to Frankfort in the state it is in now. Mary would question my responsibility. You and America will start work on it this afternoon."

"But, Aunt Henrietta, we were just getting to..." Catherine stopped. She wanted to think up a good excuse for not working on it, but seeing the worry frown on her aunt's face, decided not to push for a concession. "Yes, Auntie. We will do our best."

"See that *you* do the embroidery. America can teach you the stitches and plan the letters and decorations. But this sampler is to show your sewing skills."

"Yes, ma'am." Catherine was already preoccupied thinking how America's time with her would change to accommodate Henrietta's directive.

"Aunt Bette will be checking."

Handing America the embroidery supplies to bring to the porch, Catherine clutched her primary reader and Mother Goose book. "We will trade tasks. You will teach me how to make the stitches for the letters in my sampler. And I will listen as you read from my primer, helping you over the hard parts." Catherine assumed her role as young mistress giving orders to her slave.

"Yes, Miss Catherine." As befitted her station, America did not question the obvious change. Besides, she was anxious to try reading complete thoughts put into sentences. To lighten the mood, she offered a poser. "I spy with my little eye a magic black writing slate turning into white linen fabric. Its frame begins with the letter *H*."

"Oh, America! *H.* Hand? Holder? Hoop! Hoop! An embroidery hoop! Yes. Helpful, too!"

"The silk embroidery thread will be our limestone chalk chunks. I will clear away any mistakes or misshapen stitches just as I cleared the chalk dust." America was pleased to be helpful.

Catherine's sampler lessons proceeded. Her running stitches were fairly straight, as were the backstitches. The split stitches took some getting used to, but Catherine persevered to reign over their production along with the satin stitch. Her challenge was to conquer the stem stitch which was so important to make curves in letters *B, C, D, G, J, O, P, Q, R, S,* and *U.*

"Miss Catherine, you will need to practice the stem stitch and those letters before we go to the sampler." America was a polite but firm instructor. "I can give you hints about sewing like you do with reading." *Yes! Even though there is a color difference, we will be almost on equal terms-true friends. She can teach me and I can teach her.*

"That pleases me, America." Catherine felt happy for the first time that afternoon. "I'm afraid I will be the poorer student, though. I just don't see how someone can spend hours sewing-and enjoy it."

"Sewing is just telling the needle what to do. Don't let it be the master."

"How do you do that?" Catherine whined, looking at her sorry attempt at the stem stitch. Her letters on the fabric scraps were shaped correctly, but the challenge was to embroider them in the same size and in a perfectly straight line on the sampler. Showing more patience than she felt, Catherine practiced eleven stem curves, left and right, before stopping for the day. The last ones showed her developing skill.

"Well, I've done enough for this afternoon. We will look at Mister McGuffey's primer for a while." She opened the book and turned past the instruction pages. "Here are words and sentences we can start with. See the picture?" As Catherine pointed and read each word on the list, America repeated it. "Now, see if you can read the story." America did. At first it was rough going as she sounded out the letters. When the meaning of the seven-sentence story was evident, America's confidence grew. She read the words smoothly, as if she had memorized the piece which, indeed, she had. The smile on her face illuminated the pride and satisfaction inside.

The girls sat on the porch each afternoon for the rest of the month, sharing lessons in sewing and reading. Trying to master the French-knot stitch which requires two hands, Catherine accidentally sewed the practice cloth to the skirt of her own dress. Now, she would have to cut out the embroidery thread at each French knot she had sewn to free the scrap from her skirt. *How tedious!*

Catherine reached for her scissors.

"Miss Catherine, do you plan to cut the thread at each stitch?"

"Yes." Catherine plainly did not delight in the task ahead. *I'll never get the sampler finished by the end of summer!*

"You could just cut the knot you began with and slowly, gently pull the thread through each stitch. It will save most of the precious floss."

Catherine sighed. *She is right.*

Following America's suggestion, Catherine saved most of the thread and prepared to start over.

"Miss Catherine, you have to hold the piece in your hands. Do not put it on your knees."

"I know. Aunt Henrietta has told me that. It just seems I can control the needle easier when I use both hands which means I have to place the fabric in my lap," Catherine said. "And the needle hurts my finger every time I have to push on it to get it through the cloth!" She shook her hand in the air.

"Miss Catherine, you are bigger than a little needle," America reminded her. "Use your silver thimble to protect your finger. Thimbles are just tools to help you work a good piece of fabric."

"Well, I'll keep trying." Catherine surreptitiously wiped her hot, damp hands on her petticoat. "But it seems that my fingers turn into thumbs. And, it is so hot. I have a difficult time holding onto the needle."

❦ ❦ ❦

"Merry, Merry, not contrary, how does your garden grow?" Jeremiah Murphy entered the backdoor of his modest home. It was their usual greeting to each other. He waited for America's response.

"With silver bells, and magic spells, and bright colors all in a row." Their call and response never failed to make America smile, as did the pleasure of her father's company, despite being his slave daughter.

That evening in the Murphy household, a supper of cornbread and collard greens seasoned with ham hocks and small onions was hastily prepared by Anne to avoid lingering near the fireplace. America had returned home earlier than usual and concocted a sweet addition to the meal: dessert in the form of baked sweet potato rounds cooling on the window ledge. She topped each slice with honey before serving them to Anne and Jeremiah.

After Jeremiah satisfied his sweet tooth with two more slices of the honeyed sweet potato, he asked about America's position as servant to Mistress Morgan.

"When I finish helping Cook and Aunt Bette each day, then Miss Catherine and I help each other." America was pleased to tell her parents of her responsibilities. "We sit on the second-floor porch each afternoon. I give her hints on embroidery, and she allows me to learn from her reading primer book. She must finish her sampler by the end of the summer, and I want to learn as much as I can by the time she leaves for Frankfort. Because of the heat, though, we did not get much done today."

"I wonder if Mistress Morgan will want to keep you on after Catherine and JW return to Frankfort." Jeremiah thought aloud. "She might not want to continue your hire."

"I have wondered about that. I would be just another house girl for the mistress when Catherine leaves." America paused, considering the question she had for her papa. "Would Master Hanna hire me?" America knew that Jeremiah would see to her best interests.

"I will send an inquiry to him." Jeremiah paused now. "You understand that, if you continue to serve Miss Catherine, you would have to live in Frankfort." His obvious statement held many implications. He frowned and looked at Mama. "You would not have the comfort of returning home each evening as so many hired slaves do here in Lexington. You would live in the servants' quarters with the other house slaves."

"Yes, Papa." America thought of Jerry. *He lives in the servants' quarters behind the Skillman house. He has the appearance of being free colored, but he is owned by Master Skillman.*

"You would be at Master Hanna's beck and call all the time." Jeremiah was not sure America was aware of the harm she might encounter. She had been lucky compared to many house girls.

"Yes, Papa." America could feel the anxiety that showed on her mama's face. "Now, I want to tell you." America cleared her throat. "A servant owned by Master Skillman, the bookseller, delivered some books for Master Morgan about a month ago. He and I have exchanged pleasantries a few times. Cook told me that Jerry-that's his name-lives in a cabin behind the Skillman house. He can read and he is strong and he is handsome! But, here is what I want to say. Night and day, Jerry has to answer to all the Skillmans' requests. He seems to be able to do it. So, living in slave quarters can be all right."

"Merry, you just do not know," Anne began. "You have never been thought of as property belonging to someone else. Your papa owns us, but he loves us. That makes all the difference. This Jerry sounds like he has made the most of his circumstances and maybe is as lucky as you have been. But most blacks do not have luck on their side."

"I will look into the feasibility of hiring you out to Master Hanna and investigate what Mistress Morgan has in mind." Jeremiah sighed, trying to ease the doubts that come with change. Proud of what America had gained so far, he was uncomfortable with what the future would bring.

As if waiting for the future to present itself, Catherine grew intent on finishing her needlework, and America studied the lesson pages of the old worn McGuffey reader. During those hot afternoons, Tucky would sprawl out beside them on the porch, her tongue lolling out to catch a cool breath. Dressed in a lightweight, white cotton muslin dress with few petticoats, Catherine always had a palmetto hand fan close by, sometimes tied to her wrist with a ribbon. America's dresses were made of printed calico, usually chosen to compliment her tawny skin tones. Sometimes she covered her hair with a kerchief.

Hopemont's lawn proved to be so dry and dusty that the dead grass crunched underfoot. Transylvania University students walking to classes, etched paths in the shade of the hickory grove that gave shelter from the hot sun. No one lingered outside. With very little cooling rain, the drought that would last until the fall had begun.

"Miss Catherine, I recited the first stanza of *Lullaby of an Infant Chief* to Master Murphy last night. He enjoyed it but wants to hear the rest. Could we work on the next stanza-about a bugle and guarding a bed?" America put down the lesson book.

"Of course." Catherine's book of poetry was never far away. "I wonder if we will ever have babies to lullaby. Doing needlework in this heat surely makes me sleepy." She sighed and opened her book to Walter Scott's poem. "Look at Tucky. She is almost ready for a nap."

Tucky perked up at the sound of her name. Then she went on guard-dog alert. A familiar figure carrying a package walked toward Hopemont and then turned toward the two-story house across Second Street. America perked up, too. *That is Jerry. What is he bringing to Master John Morgan or to Mistress Becky?*

As if he knew the girls were watching, Jerry shifted the package to lift his straw hat in greeting. "Good afternoon, Miss. Good day, America."

"Hello, Jerry. Do you have something for Cousin Becky?" Catherine displayed her status by questioning his movements. Her voice was condescending.

"Yes, Miss." Jerry answered politely, as Catherine, even though having no authority, was a white resident. That made her position appropriate to the respect he showed. "Mistress Skillman has sent items of comfort to Mistress Morgan."

Huh. Comfort. Maybe he could bring comfort to me. America silently wished.

"Do you enjoy the books Master Skillman has?" Catherine asked, remembering that Jerry knew how to read. She had softened her demeanor. "America is memorizing a poem by Walter Scott from a book that belonged to Uncle Calvin."

"I do like to read in my spare time. Books can bring comfort." His statement brought a big smile to America's face, which Jerry duly noted. He addressed Catherine. "With your permission, I will be on my way." He gave a small bow, tipped his hat again, and continued on to the Bruce house across the street.

Catherine watched him go and then whispered, "You know, America, he could help you with reading once I am gone to Frankfort."

"I had the same thought!" Pleased that Catherine supported her quest to read, America handed the poetry book to Catherine. *I wish we could truly be friends.*

"You couldn't do any better!" Catherine paused and then read the second stanza of the *Lullaby of an Infant Chief*: "O fear not the bugle, though loudly it blows,/It calls but the warders that guard thy repose;/Their bows would be bended, their blades would be red,/Ere the step of a foeman draws near to thy bed."

America listened and nodded with the rhythm of the poem, imagining a baby being frightened by the sound of a bugle. *No son of mine will be an infant chief, so I doubt if anyone would come to protect him. Color decides.*

Chapter 14
Fire!

ONE OF AMERICA'S SILENT WISHES WAS ON ITS WAY. The next week, she saw Jerry again as she made her morning walk to Hopemont. "Good morning, Jerry."

"Oh! Good day to you, America!" Jerry gave her a quick, small bow. "I have been counting through Master Skillman's inventory of new song sheets. They are not bound as books, so they have no covers." He paused for a smile. "I was just wondering what you would think of them."

America remembered her mistaken term for a book's outer binding, but she chose to be serious. "I would love to look at them. But I am not yet familiar with the printed word. Actually, I am still trying to befriend the primary books that Miss Catherine owns. When she leaves for Frankfort in August, perhaps you could help me with reading?" *There. I did it. I asked what I had been thinking of since Miss Catherine voiced her approval. And, befriending him would be nice, too!*

"Yes! Perhaps we could start right away, before she leaves. Of course, we would need to find time and a place for our lessons. I will give it some thought." Jerry's smile made him even more handsome.

"I will give it some thought, too. Thank you for agreeing to help. I must be on my way." America was so excited that shyness replaced her usual composure. Turning the corner, she had to control her skipping feet.

That very afternoon, America was sent for the first time on an errand as a trusted hired servant. Mistress Henrietta directed her to take a note to her son John at his new hemp bagging manufactory on West Main Street. As she waited for Master John Morgan to consult his brother Calvin and then compose a reply, she looked around. There was the humming of the spinning and weaving machines; the hay-like, grass smell of the processed hemp that would be converted to bagging fabric; and waves of lint and dust that wafted through the open windows. Although the office in the two-storied brick building was not clean to household standards, it was comfortable and well proportioned. It had a large table in the center of the room. *This room would be a nice place to work if I was in the business of writing and calculating. A good place to sit with Jerry and share a book. Now, how can I make that happen?*

America, as usual, first sought the opinion of her parents. "Jerry and I could offer to be guardians of the hemp stored in the building as it could burst into flames in this summer heat. Or someone might want to set fire to it. We would go there after the Morgans had closed at the end of the work day. And stay until the building cooled each evening. What do you think?"

"No." Jeremiah scratched his head.

Anne shook her head. "You would be walking back home through town in the middle of the night. Have you considered that?"

"Jerry would accompany me and see that I got home safe."

"And what about the curfew for us slaves?" Her mama's questions were practical and realistic.

88

"Merry, what do you mean to do?" Jeremiah's abrupt question caught America off guard.

"I want to spend time with Jerry, enjoying the books he can get and practice reading." America's answer reflected her wish to better herself, which she knew her papa appreciated.

"Would you tell the Morgans what you just told me?" He knew the answer.

"No. I would point out to Master John Morgan the advantages of having someone look over the hemp factory after work hours." America could tell she had not convinced Anne nor Jeremiah.

"And is that what you would be doing? Being a night watchman?" Jeremiah knew what she would say.

"Well, yes and no. We would be there to send an alarm if we saw a fire start, so it could be extinguished right away. You know, Master John Wesley Hunt's factory was burned down twice." America rationalized her response.

"But, you would be giving your attention to Jerry, not to the factory." Jeremiah smiled and then looked solemn. "When offering any service, you must be forthright with your intentions. Using the excuse of fire prevention is underhanded if not dishonest."

"Yes, Papa." America smiled now. "You are right. I want so much to keep up the reading skills I have, and I want to build on my friendship with Jerry."

"How about having Jerry come over here?" Anne suggested. "We could make room on this table for you and him to read together in the evenings, almost like Reverend Ferrill coming to visit."

"Yes. London Ferrill." America's eyes sparkled. "The preacher always has stories to tell-about our first names-London and America. Maybe Jerry's visits will be just as enlightening."

"Mind you, Jerry would have to ask Master Skillman for a pass to come here." Jeremiah asserted. "We must keep within the law and be truthful about our goals."

Plans were made.

Jerry obtained a written pass from Master Skillman, coming for an hour each evening to read a borrowed copy of the *King James Bible*. The first evening he came, he unwrapped the bound volume and laid it on the kitchen table. The frayed edges of the book demonstrated its use as a teaching tool.

"Master Skillman taught me to read with this Bible," Jerry explained. "It will not raise suspicion about my movements. It is well-known that blacks are encouraged to live by the Bible." Then he looked straight at Jeremiah. "Besides, I figure if I could learn from it, America can too."

For various reasons, the Bible captured the attention of Anne, Jeremiah, and America. It served as a supplemental reading experience for America, as Jerry pointed to the words he slowly read aloud. Of course, America had to sit close by to see the text, which pleased both participants. For safekeeping, the Bible was to remain in the Murphy household.

A week later, America cleared the table and brought out the cherished book, expecting Jerry to arrive at any minute. She stopped her humming to listen. *There is a fire somewhere!* Bells were clanging, signaling members of the fire company to report for duty. The bells also alerted all able-bodied free males to lend assistance. Jeremiah grabbed the bucket near the doorway, kept for such an emergency, shoved on his Derby hat, and stepped out for a quick scan of the skyline. Billowing brown smoke rose from the west, near the convergence of two railroad lines. He walked resolutely in that direction. *Where was Jerry?*

All thoughts of enjoying a reading lesson that evening were gone with the smoke. Anne and America watched men, sporting bowler hats for protection and heavy soled boots for stability, run westward carrying leather buckets. The drought had rendered cisterns worthless, as well as the shallow wells. Water to fight the fire would have to be drawn from the Town Branch of Elkhorn Creek or any nearby spring.

Church bells began to ring, indicating more assistance was required, usually in the form of slave gangs and overseers. Mother and daughter stood in the backyard of their home on South Upper Street, watching the evening sky. Even though there was nothing she could do, America's imagination was at work. In a short time, the color of the smoke had changed from brown to black plumes. But soon the fire alarm bells ceased: seemingly no more help was needed. The smoke diminished to a white color as steam and ash dominated the flames which were dying from lack of fuel.

Weary, soot-blackened residents walked back to their homes, carrying their leather buckets. Jeremiah reported that the fire destroyed Master William Ater's hemp factory, but no other structures were harmed, thanks to the bucket brigade workers. "Black and white, slave and free, we all worked together against the insatiable flames." Jeremiah shook his head. "People of color were positioned closest to the dangerous areas."

He retired to splash water from the pitcher on the washstand Anne had ready for him in the bedroom. Then, exhausted, he fell into bed.

Jerry did not appear that evening.

The next day, Catherine was full of her version of the hemp factory fire. "Charlton and Thomas and Key and I walked down toward Johnny and Calvin's new factory to see the fire. It could have spread to their buildings, but the firemen used the new pump to put it out before it could go any further. Poor old Mister Ater frantically carried his papers and books out before the flames reached them. He returned to the burning building three times before a fire official had to stop him!"

"Looks like his slaves would tote those things out." America reflected on the action. "Maybe he did not trust them to get the necessary, most important papers, though."

"They probably could not read anyhow." Catherine dismissed America's thought. "The most horrifying spectacle was the slaves lined up to pass buckets full of water from the creek to the water pump. They were forced to heave the water into the water pump that had been driven to the side of the burning building. The light of the fire on their faces showed the terror of the heat and sound and smoke. They had no hats or boots for protection and many had shed their shirts. One slave threw a bucket of water on a fellow worker who had dropped to his knees in exhaustion. The overseer, standing at a safe distance, flicked a long whip near him as warning."

"Did he get up?" America was worried it might have been Jerry.

"No." Catherine frowned in irritation at the second interruption. "A black figure stepped up to the exhausted slave and stood next to him, grabbing each full bucket as it was handed over. By taking the exhausted slave's place to haul the heavy bucket of water into the pump, the black man gave the slave some relief. The slave stayed on his knees but was clearly grateful for the respite. The rhythm of the work was not broken, and they continued like that until the slave signaled he was ready to press on. It was only when the black man turned from his task that I recognized him. It was Jerry."

That evening, America, preparing for Jerry's arrival, asked Jeremiah if he had seen Jerry at the fire. "Yes, Merry." Pushing his comfortable, upholstered chair away from the heat of the fireplace, he continued. "Elijah Montague, the city's night watchman, kept close by him.

Jerry had to ask permission of Montague before stepping closer to the burning building. He helped a slave weakened by the labor of heaving the buckets of water."

"Miss Catherine told me that she saw Jerry helping another slave for a while." America paused. "I wonder what he and Mister Montague..."

At that moment, Jerry knocked at the kitchen door. Anne lifted the netting fabric, allowing Jerry to step through the door opening. She dropped the screening fabric to stare at him. Jeremiah and America followed her gaze. Jerry was worn out. His face, hands, and clothes were clean, indicating his half-hearted attempt to look presentable. A wet substance was smeared on his singed hair and face. Although his hands were roughed up and somewhat swollen, they did not appear to be burned.

"Good evening, everyone," Jerry began. "Well, you can guess where I was last evening!" His laugh turned into a coughing bark, and his hands went to his chest in a self-hug. The grin faded from his wet face.

"Jerry. What did you do?" It was all America could get out. She seemingly had lost her breath as Jerry coughed.

"What have you put on your hair and face?" Anne sniffed and blurted the question.

"Honey." Jerry smiled at her. "It soothes and heals. I have used it before: takes away the stink of the fire, even though it is a little messy."

"That is good to know." She inspected his face more closely. "I will have to store some away for just that purpose."

"I saw you with Mister Montague," Jeremiah broke in. "What did he want?"

"He was going to take me to jail." Jerry shrugged his shoulders. "He saw me running away from the Ater factory as the smoke billowed up: thought he was catching an arsonist red-handed. In fact, I was running toward the

Independent Fire Company on Broadway to report the fire."

"But he didn't believe you." America's voice was flat. She folded her arms.

"If he had not delayed me, I truly feel the firefighters would have set up the alarm sooner." He shrugged his shoulders again, wincing at the pain in his back.

"But he did not take you to jail," America calmly observed.

"Only because Master Morgan rushed up to inform him that he had sent me. He pointed out that time was wasting. Master Morgan himself ran to ring the first fire alarm bell while Mister Montague checked my pass from Master Skillman." Jerry's voice indicated his frustration.

"Do you know how the fire started?" Jeremiah was asking for information, although it sounded like he was questioning Jerry's actions.

"Sparks from the railcars. I had delivered a note from Master Skillman and was waiting for Master Morgan's reply. I looked over to see the railcars slow down to the Ater factory. Cinders and smoke and sparks were flying from the chimney stack of the engine just like rain." He looked heavenward. "If only it had been rain. Anyhow, in this heat, a fire was bound to happen. Daniel, a mechanic at the Morgan factory, saw what I saw, too. We pointed that out to Master Morgan about the same time a bale of bagging burst into flame. The three of us ran across the tracks to Mister Ater's factory. Master Morgan yelled to get the attention of the slaves and then called to me to run to the fire company on Broadway. That is when Mister Montague stopped me." Jerry let out a big sigh that turned into a deep cough.

"Master Morgan must have put him straight." America was somewhat proud of her connection to the revered Morgan family.

"You would think that, but Mister Montague required a written statement from Master Skillman attesting to my reliability. And he wanted the reason for me being near the Ater factory. Today, Master Skillman personally handed him the statement before Mister Montague would agree to dismiss me." A dry hacking bark escaped from his mouth. "This morning when I asked him to write the note, I could tell that Master Skillman was sorely vexed."

"Yes. You were following orders," Jeremiah, always a law-abiding slave owner, pointed out. Color decides. "I am sure Mister Montague felt he was doing the same. Sometimes, safety and common sense fly out the window when harsh rules walk in the door."

"I would like to get on with Matthew's story in the Bible book." Anne voiced her wish for normalcy. "King Herod had started the search for the child born in Bethlehem. Jerry, are you up to reading to us?" She moved the conversation away from Jerry's difficulties in Lexington to the difficulties of the young family in the Bible. "The wise men had departed and King Herod just ordered all the children less than two years old in Bethlehem to be killed."

"And Mister Burns will see to the child's rescue!" America laughed and then gave a reason for the name. "Mister Burns can be our special name for you." When Jerry raised his singed eyebrows and patted his fire-damaged hair, America went on. "We cannot call you Mister Honeytop or Mister Readmore."

"Mister Burns I will be, then!" Jerry looked at the three of them. "Now, what will be a special name for you, America?"

America looked at Jeremiah and Anne, silently seeking approval from her parents. "I already have one that only Mama and Papa use. Now, you will know it." America stated. "In this house, I am known as Merry—short for America."

Chapter 15
Hired out

"AMERICA, MASTER SKILLMAN IS GOING TO HIRE ME OUT."
Jerry stopped her on the street as she walked to Hopemont
one morning about a week later.

"Oh, no!" America saw the pain on Jerry's face. It was
not caused by the heat from his burns. It came from the
understanding that he was treated as chattel to be bought,
sold, or rented. "Why?" she asked. "Why would he do
this?"

"He is getting old, already retired from his publishing
and book business. I was very helpful in that part of his
life. Now..." Jerry's cough had not gone away.
Interrupting his speech, it ended with a gasp. "I guess he
can make money by hiring me out."

"Do you know who will lease you?" America was as
curious as she was disturbed that the book-sharing
sessions would more than likely cease. *Besides, Jerry is a
kind, wonderfully handsome acquaintance! I hope he will not be
lost to me!*

"No, not for sure. Master Skillman's cousin has a farm
in Bourbon County. He was my owner before Master
Skillman. He came for a visit last week. He sent Master a
thick letter afterward."

"You think the letter had a contract for your hire?" America remembered she could not read the contract that Jeremiah and Master Morgan signed. *Jerry could read it if he laid eyes on it. But, what difference would it make? The agreement would be between Master Skillman and his cousin! Jerry would not have a say in the terms of it.*

"Probably." Jerry studied America closely. His face revealed he had made a decision to tell her. "I have ties to that farm."

"Well, Mister Burns, are you going to tell me?" America tried to be lighthearted, but she worried all the same. *Ties? A girlfriend? A wife? How could that be?*

"Master John Skillman owns my mother and brother as he owned me," Jerry paused to let America absorb the facts. "When I was about twelve years old, Master John sold me to Master Abraham Skillman. I was picked because I was teachable and trainable. Master Abraham needed a servant to help him with his book business. Master John needed money to expand his farm to grow hemp."

"A business transaction." America knew.

"That is what all slave sales are." Jerry swallowed once. "I just did not have to stand on an auction block as chattel to be stared at and argued over by a crowd of slave buyers. Master Abraham Skillman has promised that he will not sell me, and I believe him. I am grateful that he taught me to read."

"Yes, Jerry. I am grateful that you are helping me read."

"Merry, I would like nothing more than to read along with you. That will stop if I am sent to Master John's farm." Jerry looked down at his hands for a moment. When he looked at America again, his face showed the frustration and sorrow of his circumstances.

"You have no say in what is to happen. I am sorry for that. But, you will be with your brother and mama. That should be a solace." America searched for words of comfort.

"We have been separated for about ten years now. I do not know how it will be. If I go to Master John's farm, I expect to be working in the fields." Jerry coughed after a long sigh.

"None of us knows what the future will bring. But, you should be able to rely on your relatives if they are anything like you." America paused and looked away to keep the lump in her throat from rising up to disturb her voice. "When Miss Catherine goes back to Frankfort, Papa will start looking for another owner to hire me."

"It is good to know that your papa has your best interests, even if he does own you."

"At least, I can talk with Master Murphy about where I will go." America placed her hand on his arm, feeling the heat. "I will miss Mister Burns!" She whispered, "Mister Jerry Burns. That will be my name for you. I hope you will agree to call me Merry Murphy."

Jerry whispered back, "With pleasure, Miss Merry Murphy!"

A modest looking buggy pulled by a work horse and driven by a farm slave made its way down the street. The sight was a reminder to Merry and Jerry of their individual responsibilities. With no more conversation than a wave of their hands, they went their separate ways.

The future came sooner than expected. Jerry arrived at the Murphy kitchen two days later, carrying a fabric-covered parcel and wearing a sorrowful look on his still-healing, honey-smeared face. He placed the bundle on the table that had been cleared for the evening. Colorful printed cotton squares, smelling musty from long-term storage, were inside the stained, threadbare piece of muslin. Clearly, the material had been packed for future stitching into a quilt. "Mama gave me this packet when I left the farm those many years ago. She told me that she did not have time to work on a quilt, that I could use the unfinished fabric pieces as a pillow. It was all she had to give me as a remembrance." Jerry swallowed a few times, and then a slight cough escaped.

"That is a comforting keepsake, Jerry," America responded. *Why did he bring the fabric pieces here? Seems he would be taking them back to her if he was going back to Master John Skillman's.* "Do you know where Master Abraham is sending you?"

"Yes. I will be returning to the Skillman farm in Bourbon County. I do not know if Mama will be there or if Master John sold her away." He paused and collected himself. "If she is still there, she might not have the time or energy to make this into a quilt. I think you could, Merry. I would like to leave this as a remembrance of me." He smiled. "A color-filled unfinished quilt presenting future possibilities. That is just what it was when I left Mama."

Future possibilities! He must think we will be seeing more of each other! "I will take good care of the pieces, Mister Burns!" America could not keep the smile from invading her dark brown eyes. "I wonder if your mama had a plan for these pieces."

"Probably not," Anne broke into their conversation. "When you work in a farm kitchen, your plan is to survive the last meal in order to prepare for the next. Jerry, did you know your mama very well?" Before he had a chance to reply, she continued, "On Master Henry's farm, the babies and small children were seen after by slave mammies. The only time the mamas saw their children was at night when they fed them and tucked them into bed."

Jerry nodded. "My brother Charles helped raise me more than Mama. But I knew that she loved me." He seemingly did not want to dwell on his life on the farm. "Now, I would like to read as much as I can tonight because I need to return the Bible to Master Skillman. I will be leaving tomorrow for Master John's farm." Jerry opened the book as America drew in a surprised gasp.

After listening to the travails of Jesus in Matthew's scripture, the Murphy family said their goodbyes to Jerry. "I will sew a star in the center of your quilt," America told him. "When you look up at the night sky each evening, think of me. And, I will do the same."

"We can wish on the same North Star together, although we will be apart." Jerry gave America a quick kiss on her cheek and then stepped away.

"Goodbye, Mister Jerry Burns!" America called.

"Goodnight, Miss Merry Murphy!"

The next day America told Catherine that Jerry was being hired out to Master Skillman's cousin in Bourbon County. "More than likely he will be working in the hemp fields as this is the time to cut stalks. He will not be reading much, Miss Catherine."

"I am sorry to hear that. Did he help you with any books?" Catherine was preoccupied with other things but wanted to appear supportive.

"Yes, Miss Catherine. He had been coming over in the evenings and reading aloud as I looked at the words on the pages. Now, those times will be gone." America sighed. She knew that she would miss the company of the handsome young man as much as his reading assistance.

"Well, it cannot be helped." Catherine tilted her head, thinking. "I just wonder if his master was punishing Jerry by hiring him out now because of the trouble at the time of the hemp factory fire."

That statement surprised America, especially since Catherine had witnessed Jerry's kindness to the exhausted slave. Catherine seemed to be repeating what she had heard rather than relying on the truth as she saw it. *That captain of the night watch, Mister Montague, must be behind that reasoning. He probably made up a story to justify wasting time when the fire was underway.*

"Miss Catherine, it could be Master Skillman sent him away because he thought Jerry might be hampered in the future by the city's slave codes. I just wish I had more time to enjoy his company and learn more." *There. That should be truthful and still ignore the white folks' gossip. Why spread false rumors to rationalize uselessness?*

"Well. Mister Montague did see him running from the fire. That is troublesome, especially to witness a black running down the street. You never can be too cautious when it comes to fire, especially at times like these!"

"Yes, Miss Catherine. The weather is so awfully hot and dry. Things can catch fire easily." *Including the heat of distrust!* Both girls knew that the catch phrase 'times like these' was about masters fretting over slave rebellion, not the condition of the weather.

"Can't be helped," Catherine repeated.

The hot, dry days of August settled over Lexington, turning kitchen gardens into deserts and dirt streets into dustbowls. When America finished her household duties each day, the girls sat on the second-floor porch with Tucky lolling on the shade-cooled floor between them. A side table held some of Catherine's favorite books as well as the embroidery supplies, replacing the basket of teaching materials that had been stored under the pantry window. A companionable silence replaced idle talk as each labored on her selected task: Catherine stitching her sampler and America studying the McGuffey lesson book.

"Miss Catherine, would you read the Walter Scott poem about the infant chief?" America indicated a break might relieve the creeping boredom of their work in the sweltering heat. "I want to make sure I have it correct so I can say it from memory."

"All right, America." She found the passage and began reading aloud as America listened and nodded with the rhythm. They ended up speaking the third stanza together: "Oh hush thee, my baby, the time soon will come/when thy sleep shall be broken by trumpet and drum/Then hush thee, my darling, take rest while you may/for strife comes with manhood, and waking with day."

"Thank you, Miss Catherine." America was solemn as she took the book from her young mistress and traced Walter Scott's words, mumbling them from memory. She placed the book back on the table. "I think I have it well enough. The printed word has meaning for me now. I feel that I can almost read most anything in print."

The pensive look on America's face confused Catherine. The moment should have been joyous. However, she did not question America's attitude at the time, but attempted to lighten the conversation. She announced, "Speaking of reading, I caught Tucky chewing on a book yesterday."

"Oops! What did you do?" America was obviously quite willing to consider things in a happier frame of mind.

Catherine smiled. "I took the words right out of her mouth!"

Even though America laughed, the mood had not shifted. Uncertainty dominated the afternoon, and heat enforced the decrees.

For a few days in August, when the temperature got above the hundred-degree mark, Catherine ignored her sampler chore in an effort to stay cool. Thoughts about returning to Frankfort came back to her just like the heat of the day ebbed and flowed around her. She closed her folding fan for emphasis. "Oh, America, I dread going back. Hattie will be there in all her cowering ignorance!"

America cringed. *Well, she was raised to be that way!* "I wonder what she would be like if she was not a slave."

Catherine stared at America. "How can you even consider that possibility?"

"She is a person with feelings and hopes and dreams." America knew she had invaded Catherine's sense of decorum. "Maybe she learned that being meek was the best way to get along in this world." *Color decides.*

"Well. It just sets me wrong to have her bowing and scraping in my presence. I need a mannerly, resourceful, optimistic servant-like you." She studied America's face.

America gave no hint of her mindset because she didn't know what to think. What she did know was that she missed Jerry. As a slave, he was her equal besides the fact that he was well-read. She wanted to see him every day. On the other hand, Catherine was usually pleasant to be around even though they could never be equal. Catherine seemed to care for America, she was generous with her knowledge of reading, and she appreciated her servant's abilities and talents. The tawny-skinned girl let out an appreciative sigh. "Thank you, Miss Catherine."

"Aunt Mary and Uncle John will be coming tomorrow to make final preparations for JW and me to move back to their home." Catherine straightened her shoulders and gave a nod. "I will ask Uncle John if he would hire you as my personal maid."

"Mistress Henrietta holds my contract. But I am happy that you will speak in my favor." America gave her a short unexpected bow.

Chapter 16
Jerry found a way

AS IT TURNED OUT, THE MORGAN-HANNA CONNECTIONS decided to economize concerning America's hire: Jeremiah Murphy had increased the payment required for an extension of her employment. Mistress Henrietta, though pleased with the companionship America provided for Catherine, decided that a full-time servant was not needed once Catherine left for Frankfort. John Hanna said that he already owned a servant for Catherine who would see after her needs. When America learned of the decision, she was relieved, but somewhat anxious about her future.

What came next was a pleasant surprise.

"Merry, Merry not contrary. Here is something for you." Jeremiah rhythmically sang out a revised beginning of their usual greeting and then searched through the inside pocket of his jacket. He pulled out a folded paper. America's name was on the outside fold. "It came from a Mister Samuel Crocket at Willow Valley Farm." Jeremiah enthusiastically prompted the confusion and suspense.

"Papa, who is Mister Crocket, and where is Willow Valley Farm?" America had no idea.

"Willow Valley Farm is in Bourbon County." Jeremiah was teasing.

"The only person I know in Bourbon County... Oh, Papa let me see what it is!"

He handed her the paper. "This was inside a larger wrapper addressed to me. Mister Crocket wrote a note explaining that he agreed to post it so that I would give it to you. And, so I have."

America immediately unfolded the brown paper. She saw the scratchy handwriting, wondering if she could make sense of it, and looked at the bottom of the letter to see who wrote it. She let out a squeal.

Miss Merry Murphy, Mama and Charles are still here. I work in the hemp field and see after the horses. I am to drive various transport as becomes necessary. I made the acquaintance of Mister Samuel Crocket, a school teacher, here to educate the master's children. He agreed to post this letter under his name. I trust that you are safe and happy. Give my regards to Master Murphy and know that I remain your abiding friend, Jerry Burns

"Oh, Papa!" America smoothed the rough paper as if caressing the words. "Jerry found a way to..." She could not finish the sentence. *He is safe, his mama and brother are with him, and Mister Crocket helped! And he will drive transport! Oh, the possibilities!*

Anne smiled as Jeremiah grinned at Merry twirling around the room clutching the prized page.

The hot, dry weather remained like an overbearing guest, spreading weariness and gloom. Catherine finished her sampler but took no joy in its completion. America mastered the McGuffey's lesson book but desired the skill of penmanship. Even Tucky was somewhat subdued.

The day came for young mistress and slave to say goodbye. "America, I will miss you." Catherine swallowed the lump in her throat. The girls lingered on the second-floor porch, America placing the books and sewing supplies in a large basket as Catherine looked over the porch railing. The sampler had been packed in one of the trunks. Aunt Mary and Uncle John had arrived in their coach to accompany Catherine and JW's move. Servants stowed the filled trunks and carpetbags as the family said their goodbyes.

"I will miss you, Miss Catherine." America replied as she solemnly faced her young mistress.

Catherine first placed her hands on America's shoulders, then stretched her arms for a sisterly embrace. America returned the hug.

"I do not know when I will see you again." She had a sorrowful look on her face, reminding America of that same look when they first met. At that time, Catherine was mourning the loss of her mother. Now, it was the loss of an unorthodox friendship.

"Miss Catherine, our paths might cross. Who knows what the future will bring?" America wanted to be positive.

"Catherine!" JW's voice preceded him as he galloped up the back stairs. "You must come down! Aunt Mary and Uncle John are waiting!"

Following Catherine and JW who carried Tucky, America brought the large basket downstairs. She placed the sewing items and two books from Uncle Calvin's collection in Catherine's carpetbag. The McGuffey's reader was to remain at Hopemont.

The two adults in the coach watched as Aunt Henrietta kissed Catherine and JW goodbye. Brother waited until sister settled into their back-facing seat, and then he handed Tucky over to her before getting in himself. Everyone waved and fluttered handkerchiefs until the four horses pulling the coach turned the corner onto Main Street then on to Frankfort.

America assumed duties as a full-time house servant until her contract expired at the end of the month. At Aunt Bette's suggestion, though, Mistress Henrietta decided to direct America to see after the youngest children in the household, Thomas and Key Morgan. America was already aware of the rambunctious boys as they played in and around the house. "I wish to see how you get along with them," Henrietta explained as she placed a hand on the shoulder of each son. "Since Johnny is busy with his own business and Tommy is away in St. Louis and Catherine and JW are now gone to Frankfort, Tom and Key have no one to occupy their time." Each boy showed courtesy and good manners by nodding at America, but they were obviously anxious to be elsewhere. America's status was clearly below theirs.

Does she want me to be a playmate? What will I do with them? What will they do with me? "Yes, Mistress Morgan. I will see how I can keep them occupied." *Mistress must be pleased with how I managed Catherine. She wants to see how I would handle her own sons.* Searching for inspiration, America looked through the window of the pantry. It was sheltered by the porch roof. *Shade. We must keep out of the hot, glaring sunlight.* "Would you like to play follow the leader?" She looked at Tom and then at Key.

"All right, America," said Tom. "The leader needs to commence with orders."

"Yes, Master Tom." America saluted him. "Here is a suggestion: Find a path that is covered from the sun. Everyone marches single file through shade."

"I will be leader. Everyone must do what I do." Key grabbed a nearby fancy walking stick and waved it as a drawn sword to lead the way. Aunt Bette immediately traded it for a short broom stick and stood back for his march through the side door. Tom and America followed behind.

Key led them past the kitchen and carriage buildings, through the sycamore and locust grove, and circled back to the north side of Hopemont. A low stone fence guarded the dry non-functioning well in the yard. It was there that Key called a halt to the march in order to sit on the cool stones in the shade of the three-story house. After a brief rest, America suggested that they visit the pantry for a refreshing drink of cool tea.

Keeping the young Morgan brothers occupied during the hot August days became a challenge for America. She superintended their slingshot practices, quoit games, toy soldier battles, and even took part in their marbles competition. Her favorite pastime with Tom and Key was listening to the stories they read aloud. Though not as proficient as Catherine, Tom was the more fluid reader, especially of the Walter Scott books that his father owned. Possessing a melodious voice, he read the poems with grace and authority.

The last day of August dawned bright and hot. America walked to Hopemont along hard clay-baked streets, covering her face to avoid the swarms of gnats from the dusty wind. The drought continued in full force. Even the usually boisterous boys were subdued in the dry heat of the day. This was her last day of hire at Hopemont.

She said goodbye to Tom and Key and then bid farewell to Aunt Bette and Cook. That was difficult. She had learned the manners and necessary skills of a proficient house servant from Aunt Bette. Cook, by example, had shown her efficient means of food preparation. Together they were America's support in the world of white authority. To her surprise that afternoon, Jeremiah appeared at the office door of the residence asking to speak with Mistress Morgan. He had come to remind her of the contract and request payment the next day. America was summoned to the office.

"America, I have been pleased with your work in this household," Mistress Henrietta announced. "I no longer require your services, but wish you well. You have been very helpful to my family." She extended her hand as a goodbye gesture.

"Thank you, Mistress Morgan. I have learned a great deal here." America dipped a curtsy and touched Henrietta's hand in subservience.

"Now, Mister Murphy," Henrietta turned to him. "You can expect remuneration tomorrow as agreed. I will send my son Tom to your livery with the payment. If I find that a hired house servant is needed in the future, I will seek out your business."

"I would like that very much, Ma'am," Jeremiah nodded as he picked up his bowler hat. "If you will excuse me, I must be on my way. Good day." He exited, giving America a smile, and closing the door as he went.

And that was that.

Chapter 17
Changes

"MERRY, MERRY, NOT CONTRARY, how does your garden grow?" Papa greeted America when he came in the kitchen door at the end of his work day. He hung his Derby hat on the peg next to the door and immediately shed his black wool jacket.

"With silver bells, and magic spells, and bright colors all in a row." The call and response gave America a sense of comfort, but her mind was on future prospects. "Papa, have you found anyone to hire me?" America put down the bedsheet she was marking with small embroidered letters. It was a help for Anne when sorting laundry to be able to identify ownership of items. Since America was now familiar with the alphabet and had taught her mama the letters for each client, she could sort the pieces quickly.

"Master David Tanner asked about a house girl. He lives in Clark County."

"Do you know him? Does he have a farm?" America was cautious.

"I know he has a farm to grow hemp and raise livestock." Jeremiah eased into the side chair that was now placed near the open window. A hot breeze stirred the air in the kitchen and then escaped to tease the curtains in the middle room of the small house. "He was in town today and put up his horse and buggy at my livery while he attended to business. When he came back, he spoke of hiring a servant rather than buying one."

"It seems more owners are doing that," Anne said. "It leads me to hope that white folk will come to think slavery is not necessary."

"Slave owners will do whatever it takes to make a profit or make a good impression of success, Anne." The prickly heat and meager income from his recent business dealings brought Jeremiah to a low simmer: he was in no mood to mince words or stir up a debate about slavery. "This drought has damaged crops and diminished livestock. People are just not spending much these days."

"Maybe that will keep slave catchers away." Her kidnapping was a constant concern for America. "If they cannot sell any slaves, they may not try to steal any."

"I would not count on that, Merry. They would just sell for a lower price." Jeremiah trembled at the notion. Wanting America to be safe, he emphasized the importance of being on guard, however troublesome it made her life. "I need to find out about Master Tanner. His farm is named Pleasant Green Hill and, among other livestock, he said he breeds horses."

"And horses are your business." America wondered if Master Tanner thought of slaves and horses as chattel to be used as he wanted.

"I will visit the farm," Jeremiah continued, "to view horses I may purchase for the livery and get an idea of how Pleasant Green is run. You know, if you are hired, you will have to live in the quarters with the other slaves."

"Papa, unless I am free, I will have to live that way." America did not mince her words either. "The slave I live with now is Mama! Since we are colored, we dwell in cottages and cabins and quarters and cubbyholes."

"Yes, Merry." Frustration showed on Jeremiah's face. He removed his sweat-soaked black tie and unbuttoned his form-fitting waistcoat. He took a sip of sweet water from the glass Anne had placed nearby. By silent observation, both mother and daughter knew he was about to say something of consequence.

"You have wondered why I have not set you free." He cleared his throat. "Maybe it is my own self-interest. I will admit that you have made my life fuller and more comfortable." He turned to Anne. "If I had not bought you, I would not have had the joy of begetting you, America." He nodded to his daughter. "I love you both. I love this peaceful, welcoming home you have made." Jeremiah looked around the kitchen.

America and Anne fanned themselves, waiting for more explanation. "Maybe it is because you earn money for me. Goodness knows, you are both conscientious and honest. My customers are always satisfied, and I rely on their good words about you to generate more work which turns into more income for me."

"Yes, Papa. We know that." America was showing her impatience.

"Did you know that owning slaves is a sure sign of success? When I told a stranger that my girl was hired out as a house servant to the Morgans, he took notice. When someone asked about the style and tidiness of my appearance, I replied that my house servant took care of my clothes and hat and shoes. I got admiring glances. On the government rolls, a person's property value is listed for tax purposes. I own both of you, this house, and my livery stable. I pay the taxes, so I am a successful businessman."

"Well, Papa, Mama and I will never be successful businessmen." America was not interested in property or taxes. As a colored female, any business was out of the question for her. "Why are we still bonded to you?"

"The main reason, I guess, is that I am afraid I will lose you." He sighed.

"What!" Confused, America saw an almost defeated look on Jeremiah's face.

"If you were free, where would you go? How would you live? Most free coloreds in this town have a rough life. They have to arrange for their own food, shelter, and clothing while they work under slave conditions."

"But they take pride in the fact that no one owns them or their children!" America spoke insistently, wanting Jeremiah to understand her yearning to be free. She glanced at her mama, who avoided her look. "Besides, we could just live here with you, earning money for our shelter, food, and clothing as we do already. The difference is the signed paper showing that we are free, instead of permission papers and passes."

"There is a big difference."

"What?" America had to know.

"The Fugitive Slave Law." As Jeremiah said this, he disappeared into the middle room to open a trunk that held a box of documents. "Ah, here they are. These prove my ownership."

"How is that going to help?"

"Merry, if you run away or are kidnapped," Jeremiah put up his hands to stop America's interruption. "Now, hear me out. Slave catchers will kidnap or pull all sorts of shenanigans to convince you to run away. These papers of entitlement give me the legal right to track you down. If I could *not* prove that I own you, no authority would assist me."

At a loss to fully understand what Jeremiah said, America wanted proof. "What are those papers?"

"This one is my receipt for buying your mama. Here, I will read it: "Received of Jeremiah Murphy Two hundred fifty dollars in payment for a negro girl named Anne, about 18 years old, brown complexion, light eyes, likely skills, which negro I warrant sound in mind and body and a slave for life. The title I will forever defend. Fayette County, Kentucky, May 18, 1830 — Henry Wickliffe.'"

"Oh, Mama." America read the words as Jeremiah pointed to them.

"And here is your registration paper, America." Papa unfolded and read it aloud: "'This is to certify that a female infant named America born on November 7, 1836, whose negro Mother is named Anne, aged now about 2 years old a native of Lexington, has been duly registered at this office as the property of Jeremiah Murphy. Signed, J. C. Rodes, clerk Fayette County Court May 1, 1838.'"

"You mean to tell me if that man, James McMillen, *had* stolen me…" America began.

"A constable would not have started looking for you until I had shown him the registration paper. We were lucky that Eli came along to distract that scoundrel. Slaves have been kidnapped right and left. That Fugitive Slave law paper, passed four years ago, protects my rights to find you."

"What if I just ran away? Like Joseph and Mary and baby Jesus fled to Egypt in the Bible story? Maybe Jerry could protect me as we make our way north across the river and into Canada." America watched to verify what her parents thought of an escape.

"Oh. Oh. Oh. No, America!" Anne couldn't reason with that possibility other than voice an emotional disapproval.

"Mama, I am just thinking of all the ways I can better myself. You and Papa have helped me along, but it seems that Jerry would be willing to take me further. Right now, I have no plans to run away, nor the stomach for it, but I want to think of all possibilities. I do not even know if he and I could pair up."

"Do you know that escaping from slavery is against the law?" Jeremiah blurted out.

"And, how is that, Papa?" America was surprised.

"Slave owners claim that slaves, by escaping, are actually stealing-themselves! They are taking property that belongs to the slave master." Papa shook his head. "That law will be the ruination of this state. But at least I can use it to legally protect you from being sold, if…"

"If you can convince the authorities in time to find the slave catchers," America finished his sentence in a rueful voice. She remembered Jerry running from the hemp warehouse fire. Mister Montague, the watchman, wasted precious time as the factory burned. Jerry's word was not accepted and Master Skillman had to verify the truth of the matter. Color decides.

"I will investigate Master Tanner tomorrow." Jeremiah was already weary of the frightful conversation concerning America's future.

As it turned out, his trip to Pleasant Green Hill was almost pleasant. A cooling rain shower before dawn had a cleansing effect on the dusty Winchester Turnpike. The livery-stable horse was energized by the early morning exercise and knew how to pick his way along the dry, cracked roadway. Arriving just before the noonday meal, Jeremiah took dinner with the family and observed the kindly character of the household staff. He also found an unexpected benefit in the visit: the Tanner land had been in the family for three generations.

"Master David has six slaves and two slave cabins," Jeremiah reported. "As far as I can tell, he is not in need of another house girl as his only daughter recently married. He already owns female servants who see to the needs of his wife. Mistress Tanner does set a fine table." Jeremiah paused. "Master David's nephew, Branch M. Tanner, lives in a separate house on the land and farms it independently. After dinner, I accompanied him to his home."

"You must have an opinion of the nephew's family." America picked up on his hesitancy.

"I do. Branch Tanner has a younger household with four children. His house servants seem to keep everything running smoothly, but it seems that Mistress Rebecca needs help with the youngsters. Two relatives were there today, but I do not know if they help Mistress or not. Master Branch owns one Negro man and a boy about ten years old, who work as farm servants, keeping the outbuildings and horses in order. There is just one slave cabin."

"Are his horses in good condition?" America had to ask.

"Yes. They are well taken care of. And his stable building is substantial. Maybe the man and boy live in the loft above the stalls. Master Tanner has hired help, so those slaves might sleep in the second floor of the stable."

"Do you think Master Branch would hire me as a house servant? Do you think I would do well there?" America trusted Jeremiah's business sense and his love for her.

"I thought about the situation the whole distance between Pleasant Green Hill and home. I cannot find a better position for you. Master Branch Tanner's household seems to be a good fit for your abilities and skills." Jeremiah glanced at Anne to gauge her reaction. As usual, she just showed an acceptance of the situation.

"Here is another bit of information that came to my notice. One of Master Branch's slaves is a woman they call Dicy, who is about ninety-eight years old. I do not know how she came to live at the Tanner farm, but the fact she is there indicates that the family is taking care of her."

"And the other servants must value her presence." America smiled for the first time at the information Papa brought. "She might help me adjust to life with the family."

"Now, do not get your hopes up, Merry," her mama cautioned. "It could be that because of her age and experience, she will make work more difficult for you. As the younger, more inexperienced girl, you are at a disadvantage. You need to see how she handles things with the other household servants."

"She might be like Aunt Bette, though. But that probably is not the case." America naturally understood the ins and outs of household positions and was already missing the leadership of the beloved Morgan servant. "It might be that she is just a well-liked nursemaid. I will have to step lightly until I find my place."

"So, I have determined that you would suit that work." Jeremiah made the statement, knowing that America wanted to be hired out. "The contract would be just for the last days of this year. If the circumstances warrant, we would not be bound beyond that."

His daughter would be leaving the security of the Murphy home as well as the comfort of being surrounded by hundreds of people her own race in Lexington. For the first time she would trade her city sensibilities for life in the country.

"It will be an adventure." America put on a brave face. *Jerry did not have a say, but he is living on a farm now, too.* "Papa, will you come every so often to see if they are treating me right? Perhaps you could use your livery business as an excuse."

"Oh, yes, Merry," Jeremiah answered. "I need to see after my business interests."

The following day, America learned that Jeremiah had already drawn up the contract. To her dismay, she found out that the negotiations between Jeremiah and Master Branch Tanner had been completed before he returned to Lexington. She felt somewhat betrayed by his bargaining effort, but after all, she trusted him. Deep down, she knew he had her best interests at heart: she just wanted to voice her opinion of the agreement before it was signed.

"Papa, I would like to see the contract."

"Yes, Merry. Here it is. I will point out the handwriting as I read it. Then I will put it away in the trunk with the other documents." He unfolded the paper. "It says that America-see your name-is hired as a house servant for the remainder of the year. On December 25, 1854, Branch M. Tanner will pay Jeremiah Murphy-that's my name there-the sum of thirty dollars, and the contract may be renegotiated for the next year. Board will be provided by the Tanner family, but clothing will be furnished by owner Jeremiah Murphy who is also responsible for the property tax." America viewed the contract, squinting to make out some of the handwritten provisions, before Jeremiah folded it to put away.

"Papa. I would like to send a message to Jerry. Would you help me with it? You could post it to the teacher at Master Skillman's farm, with a note that my message is for Jerry." America had become bold with her requests.

"All right, Merry." Jeremiah hesitated. "You have the use of paper, ink, and quills, but you will write the words. I will help as best as I can with spelling and penmanship. You understand, though, I am not a teacher-or a clerk."

"Papa, I am pleased that you are permitting me to keep in touch with Jerry." America gathered the writing materials and sat at the kitchen table, thinking for a long time before lettering her words:

Mister Burns, I received your note last month with heartfelt gladness. I will be at a farm in Clark County as I have been hired to Master Branch Tanner as a house girl. I trust you have made friends with the Skillman horses and your burns have healed. Grateful for your kindliness, I remain your steadfast friend, Merry Murphy

"Well, Merry," Jeremiah exhaled before saying more. "Except for the splotches and ink drips, I think you have crafted a fine letter to Jerry."

"I hope he will find a way to come visit me. If Master Skillman trusts him with the horses and has Jerry drive the carriages and wagons for him, it looks to me that he would write a pass for Jerry to come over to Master Tanner's farm." America crossed her fingers.

Papa wanted his daughter to understand the procedure. "You know that you have to get permission from Master Tanner to accept visits from Jerry."

"Yes, Papa. I will need to prove my trustworthiness first."

Chapter 18
Pleasant Green Hill Farm

AMERICA'S CONTRACTED WORK BEGAN at ten o'clock the next day. Mistress Rebecca Tanner seemed to appreciate America's arrival, as did twelve-year-old Harriet and eight-year-old Sarah. When mention was made of various undertakings, including playing school, the girls perked up. Just like the Morgan boys, though, ten-year-old Reuben would rather have been outside playing with Willie, a young Negro boy his age. Patience and good manners were evident when introductions were made. Five-year-old David just stood shyly in his older brother's shadow, listening and looking. As with the Morgans, America would divide her time between completing household chores and seeing after the children.

The farmhouse was modest compared to Lexington society standards. An enormous fireplace dominated the kitchen, the biggest, most well-used room. It housed all the food supplies, kitchen tools, and preparation areas. There was a trapdoor in the floor farthest from the fireplace that covered a small cellar room, constructed to store perishable foodstuff. In one corner was a spinning wheel and a small loom. The corner nearest the back door held a washstand and various wooden tubs for laundry. A haven for female servants, the kitchen was tidy; however,

America noticed at once that it needed more scrubbing and daily attention.

Fifty-year-old Rose was in charge as cook. Already weary from the morning's work in the hot room, she inspected America with a suspicious look, as if wondering whether this small light-skinned servant girl could help her. America understood the look. *Will I make friends with this overworked woman? Is it important that I do?*

Nina, Rose's helper, was about America's age, but much taller, darker, and heavier. She walked into the kitchen just as Rose was showing America the wash tubs and clothes horses.

"Ah, here's Nina." Rose turned to America. "Nina is a good helper. She is strong and works hard at any task until it is complete. Nina, this is America. She is hired to help Mistress Rebecca with the children and to help us with our household duties."

"Pleased to meet you." Nina dipped at her knees, then bounced up quickly when America showed her surprise. *One slave curtsying to another? Wonder what led her to behave like that?*

"I am glad to meet you." America looked her in the face. "I hope we can work together, Nina. I want to help you and Rose as best as I can." America clutched her carpetbag.

"Nina can show you the servants' quarters." Rose demonstrated her leadership.

Harriet and Sarah entered the room.

"Oh, we will show her," Harriet volunteered. Nina was quite willing to let the girls take America to the quarters. "You will share the cabin with Rose and Nina and another special person," Harriet announced as they walked toward the slave quarters. The path from the house to the cabin was freshly swept.

The cabin door stood wide open. Harriet pushed back the long piece of netting that hung from the door frame to discourage flying insects. A curtain at the only window in the cabin was pulled back, inviting any breeze to linger awhile.

"Aunt Dicy, here's our new girl." America and the sisters paused as they stepped through the doorway, allowing their eyes to adjust in the darkened room. A welcome coolness emanated from the hard-packed dirt floor.

America looked around to spot the person Harriet had addressed. What she saw was two roughly constructed bed frames, each supporting a lumpy mattress. In the center of the room stood a kitchen table, satin smooth from daily use and practical scrubbing. Two rush-bottom chairs tilted against it, seats angled downward. Hearing a creaking sound opposite the door, America spied a small dark figure slowly moving to and fro in a large rocking chair. Her wrinkled, walnut-colored skin seemed to make her a part of the log cabin that had been witness to many slave tribulations.

"This is America, Aunty. She has come to help Rose and Nina and to look after us."

"Well, that is a tall order for a short girl." Aunt Dicy looked America up and down. She set aside the shirt she was mending in the dim light from the open window. "America, you say? How old are you, girl? You look to be a half hand."

America smiled self-consciously. "I do not take up much space, but I do a full share of the work."

"I am glad to hear that. These are your quarters while you are here. You and I will be sharing the bed over there." She pointed toward the northeastern corner of the cabin. A serviceable quilt neatly covered the cornhusk mattress on the bed that was built into the wall. "Did Master Branch buy you on the auction block?" Aunt Dicy did not mince words. She sought to make acquaintances quickly. Slave life was not permanent: human chattel arrived and departed without much notice, depending on the owners' whims, economic stability, and the physical endurance of the slaves themselves.

"No, Aunt Dicy," America answered. "My master hired me out. He owns my mama and me and finds work for us. She does laundry for patrons in Lexington, and I have helped her, learning her ways."

"I heard you were a house girl for the Morgans at Hopemont." Harriet broke into the conversation. "Mother said you are well trained to help in the kitchen and take care of the children."

Feeling as if Harriet was pointing out the achievements of a prized thoroughbred, America chose to ignore the attitude behind the proprietary statement. "I did work in the Morgan household for a short time." America nodded at twelve-year-old Harriet. "I learned quite a bit from Aunt Bette and Cook." She turned to face the ninety-eight-year-old slave. "I hope to learn as much as I can from you, Aunt Dicy."

"Well, girl, my cooking and cleaning days are over." Aunt Dicy almost frowned, but then brightened at the next thought. "But I can still do some sewing, and I tend to the garden behind the cabin. Let me show you what I have grown."

Neither Harriet nor Sarah was interested in standing out in the blazing sunlight to view the kitchen garden, so they returned to the farmhouse. With that invitation from Aunt Dicy, America found a new endeavor to pursue. *I can read with the girls and learn gardening from Aunt Dicy! Jerry would like that.* The look of happy anticipation illustrated her pleasure at the prospects of working at Pleasant Green Hill.

"Why, the drought has not damaged the herbs." America squatted to touch the thyme and sage growths that were fresh but dry. She used her free hand as a visor to shield her face from the relentless sun. "What is this sturdy looking plant?" The white undersides of its pointed leaves accented the small white flowers on the stalk.

"Ahh. That is one of my favorites: mugwort. I let it grow freely in this patch because I use it for many purposes." Aunt Dicy studied America before going on. "I dry the roots and mix some with pennyrile to make an incense. And I grind some of it to flavor a drink. I boil the leaves for a tonic. And I give some of the stalks to fieldworkers to put around their waists for protection."

Protection? America was curious but did not ask. Instead, she commented on a plant she was acquainted with. "I see those pretty little chamomile flowers. They seem to like the sunshine. I know they make a good tea if you let it steep for a while."

"Yes, child," Aunt Dicy was pleased to talk about her garden. "We need to get in from the heat."

Just as they stepped through the door of the cabin, the farm bell clanged. "Time to help Rose," Aunt Dicy announced as she immediately headed for the house. "Come on, girl. The family will be there soon enough for dinner. We cannot keep them waiting."

As the two women walked to the house, they noticed Willie, the eight-year-old slave, carefully wrap the long bell rope to the post that held the old bronze bell. The clanging of the bell, which signaled the midday meal time throughout the farm, was a new chore for him. Attuned to the chimes of the clock above the mantle in the kitchen, Rose knew when to have Willie ring the farm bell.

Wordlessly, Rose handed America a white apron as soon as she stepped in the kitchen. She motioned for her to take the platter of sliced ham and the bowl of black-eyed peas to the dining room. Nina had already set the table with a homespun cloth and the common tableware the family used most days. Rose bustled in with a bowl of smothered greens, seasoned with bacon and onion bits, and a basket of cornbread muffins. Rose, Nina, and

America then withdrew to the kitchen while the Tanner family served themselves at the table. When the savory meal was consumed, Mistress Rebecca used her silver hand bell to signal that the dinner dishes need to be cleared and dessert, in the form of pie, would be served. Aunt Dicy had cut the apple pie and placed slices on smaller plates for Rose, Nina, and America to serve.

The fieldworkers spent the noon mealtime in the shade of fence line trees near the fields. They ate cornbread and bacon, supplemented by chunks of sweet potato, washed down with water Willie had brought from the deep kitchen well. With the drought, no refreshing spring water was available.

Willie had scurried back to the house to be ready to ring the big bronze farm bell again. Having weathered many seasonal changes, it had taken on a silver color. The slave boy waited at the kitchen door for Rose to direct him to ring the bell, which signaled to field hands and family to resume their activities. It was only after they cleared the dining table that Rose, Nina, Aunt Dicy, and America had their midday meal in the kitchen, which was the food left over from what had been prepared for the Tanners.

Mistress Rebecca brought in a wicker basket of clothes and linen. "America, these items need to be mended before they are washed. The necessary sewing supplies are in the drawer of the washstand. You can work on them at the times when you are not helping Rose or seeing after the children."

"Yes, Ma'am." America looked in Rose's direction.

"I will not need your help for a while." Rose nodded to her. "Nina, here can show you what is required with keeping the house presentable. You will need to see about the children's rooms, too."

"Come this way." Nina led America through the dining room into the sitting room at the front of the house. "Mistress Rebecca is particular about this room and the dining room. She wants it to be clean all the time. The breezes bring dust that covers everything, though."

America looked at the tidy surroundings. The rooms were not spotless as in the Morgan house. The fabric fittings needed laundering. "Yes. I see that. It certainly has been hot." Fanning herself, America took a quick look at the streaked mirror above the settee and the begrimed knickknacks on the mantle. *Maybe Nina just does not know how to clean things.*

Harriet appeared at the door holding a packet of papers bound with blue ribbon. Both servants stopped their inspection of the sitting room. Nina turned to dip an almost imperceptible curtsy. "Good afternoon, Miss Harriet."

Ignoring Nina, Harriet held out some of the handwritten pages to America. "I wish to show you these poems, America. They were written by Joel Tanner Hart, one of Father's cousins." She pointed to the fireplace. "He built that chimney and the one in the dining room." All three of them stepped back to look.

"He worked with masonry and wrote poetry?" America couldn't imagine why a person would do both. "I would like very much to read the poems, but I am not an accomplished reader. Would you agree to help me?"

"Oh, yes. It will be nice to read together, playing school." Harriet paused. "And here is something else." She pointed to a small marble bust on the mantle. "Cousin Joel made this bust of Henry Clay. He carved many of these small images to make money, but when he set off on his trip to Italy, he gave this one to Father."

"Oh, my! You mean he carved it out of marble?" America could not hide her admiration. Although she did not pick it up, she examined it closely.

"That plaster flower is one he did, too. Is that right, Miss Harriet?" Nina asked.

"Yes, Nina. We have to be very careful because it would break to pieces if it was accidently dropped."

With her eyes, America examined the exquisite dust-laden plaster piece. *Nina and Harriet have probably been told over and over to be careful with that.* "Is it a morning glory?"

"Yes. Cousin Joel would study something and draw sketches of it from all sides, then form it in plaster so it looked lifelike."

"Beautiful." America voiced her opinion, then realized she had spoken out of turn. *That morning glory is so fragile looking, I almost want to pick it up. The white of the plaster keeps it from looking like a real one. It is like a ghost of a morning glory. Color makes a difference.*

"But Cousin Joel wrote poetry." Harriet indicated the pages with a shake of her wrist. "Maybe we can read them together tomorrow."

"Yes, Miss Harriet," America gratefully anticipated continuing her reading education.

But the reality of life as a slave intervened.

Chapter 19
Aunt Dicy

WITH NO WARNING, A BLACK MAN JUMPED into America's path. She was on her way to the slave cabin, in the gray light of early evening. Startled, she took a few steps back, sloshing the small pitcher of buttermilk she carried and tipping the saucer of cornbread.

"Hey, girly, you hired to look after the Tanner children? Who is gonna look after you?" His voice was mocking and he seemed to dance on his toes. With his hands on his hips, he tilted his head to get a better look at her. He smirked. "Why, you are no bigger than a half hand."

Aware that he was not going to grab her immediately, America squatted to pick up the cornbread and wipe buttermilk dribbling down the metal pitcher. She covertly looked for aid. *No help coming. I will have to do something quick.* "Oh, I have spilled the buttermilk for Aunt Dicy! She is waiting for it." Showing no fear, America looked fully at his face and stood up, stretching to her tallest height.

"Well, I am waiting for some sweetness, myself," he answered. "Do you have anything for me? Or will you be my dessert?"

"Oh, you can get some in the kitchen," America appeared to be helpful, but actually was letting him know that others were nearby. "Rose and Nina might have a leftover slice of pie."

"Sounds like you have met everyone here except me."

"Yes." America did not elaborate. Out of the corner of her eye, she caught sight of Aunt Dicy.

"Well, let me introduce myself, sweet one." He hesitated. "I am Henry, a free man, newly enslaved. I see after the stock and the barn for Master Tanner."

Aunt Dicy arrived. "Huh, Henry. You are not a free man any more than I am! Never have been. America, this full hand was born a slave. He is full of himself! But he does a good job of seeing after the animals and the barn." Aunt Dicy pointed to the sizeable, well maintained two-story combination stable and storage building.

"It is good to know you, Henry." America had calmed herself enough to smile at him. *It is good to know who you are so I can look out for you!*

"You saw his son Willie working the bell at midday." Aunt Dicy was letting America know more about Henry. She wanted to smooth over the wrong impression he had given.

"Well, Aunt Dicy, Henry's greeting surprised me enough that I spilled your buttermilk and let the cornbread fall." America wanted to let both of them know Henry had not handled himself well. Still haunted by the kidnap attempt in April, she was especially sensitive to being startled by an unknown man.

"No doubt." Aunt Dicy turned to Henry. "Well, what do you say?" She treated him like a youngster. Considering their gap in ages, he was.

"I was just playing." Henry looked down, and then bobbed his head up with a defiant look at America. "You are little. Seems you would do about as much work as Willie, and he is only eight years old."

Huh. That statement cannot justify rudeness. "You need not think of work as only brute force. We are not horses."

America, inspired by the beauty of the marble bust and plaster morning glory, was more outspoken than usual. *Color is important. We need to go beyond the color barrier, though.* "Whites use us as work animals, but we do not have to be that."

"What are you saying?" Henry was confused with her statements.

"We are not work animals." America repeated her words for emphasis. "We do better using our knowledge and skills, not by acting like beasts." She stood as tall as she could on her toes. "And, even though we are both slaves, I warn you: just because I am a girl and smaller than you does not mean I should fear you!"

"Amen, child," Aunt Dicy murmured. "Now, America, we should get back to our quarters. I am hungry for that cornbread and buttermilk."

"You will be seeing more of me, sweet one," Henry displayed his masculine pride.

"At least I will not to be startled by your presence now that we understand each other."

"Yes. I will be more respectful." Henry gave a slight bow to both women and walked away.

"America, do you have a boy who is sweet on you?" Aunt Dicy asked quietly, once they were in the cabin.

"Yes." In her mind, America compared Henry to Jerry and realized how she missed him. "Why do you ask?"

"If your beau paid a visit every once in a while, and Henry met him, he would not try to pester you as I think he is planning to do." Aunt Dicy's years had served her a full measure of wisdom. "I do not know if he will try anything other than to pester, but a young girl like yourself cannot be too careful."

"My friend Jerry is hired out to a farmer in Bourbon County." America turned to search through her carpetbag for the packet of quilt pieces Jerry had given her. "I do not know if he could come over every week. I know we have to ask permission of Master Tanner for Jerry to come at all."

"Well, girl, we can think of a way." Aunt Dicy eyed the cornbread and buttermilk. "Right now, I want my supper. After I give my body some nourishment, and my mind has a chance to rest so my spirit flies free, usually an answer will come."

"Well, Aunt Dicy." Part of a solution had already occurred to America. "Master Murphy will be coming here in a week or two, to see how things are going with my hire. He can send a note to Jerry!"

"Can your Jerry read the note?" Aunt Dicy bit into a square of cornbread.

"Oh, yes. His owner in Lexington taught him to read as a help with his bookselling business."

"Girl, you are one lucky slave. You have a kind owner and a beau who can read." Aunt Dicy wasn't so much jealous as admiring of America's circumstances. "You will be free colored before you know it!"

"I am very fortunate. But I want more than this." America stopped and looked down at the muslin parcel containing Jerry's parting gift. It would be her pillow until she could work the pieces into a quilt. She did not want to reveal her innermost wishes at this time. *Can I trust her?* "Aunt Dicy, have you ever healed burns to the skin with honey?"

"Well, I have heard that it can be done. I use my own mixtures from the garden when somebody gets burned or scalded." She studied America. "There is a honey tree near one of the fields. But usually, the hands keep track of the bees and steal the honey when Master directs them to. Master and Mistress both like their honey, so there is not much of it for the taking."

"Jerry was burned fighting a warehouse fire, and he smeared honey on his skin and hair. I have not seen him since that time." The anxious look on America's face showed that she missed him, although a smile came as she held some of the fabric squares. "He gave me these fabric pieces before he left for Bourbon County. I want to sew a quilt."

"I might help you with that." Aunt Dicy wiped her supper dishes and put them on the table to take back to the house in the morning. "And maybe I can offer some suggestions on how to arrange for Jerry to pay a visit."

America did not know what to say other than to thank her elderly friend, who was presently in the process of making herself comfortable in the rocking chair. Putting a piece of dried mugwort on a small thin rock, she lit it with the flame of the only candle in the room. She placed it in the center of the wide arm of the rocking chair. The mugwort produced a thin spiral of smoke, which Aunt Dicy studied intently. She closed her eyes and sat very still.

By silently watching, America knew that Aunt Dicy was becalmed for a long time. Finally, the older woman shook herself. It was as if she had spent too much time listening.

"Girl, I see that Jerry will have a big part in your freedom, but it will be a long time coming-years. You will enjoy each other as man and wife for a short time. Both of you have had fortunate lives but will see much sorrow."

"Aunt Dicy, you saw all that by looking at the mugwort smoke?" America had never seen such thing.

"The mugwort frees my spirit so I can find the answer to my question," she said.

"What was your question? I did not hear anything." America was uncertain of Aunt Dicy's answer.

"I asked the question inside my head. I asked if you and Jerry would have a good life together and if he could help you. Basically the answer was 'yes,' but your life will be hard."

"Oh. And you got that just from the mugwort smoke."

"It took me years to know what to do to let my spirit fly free. I got impatient more often than not, and sometimes my spirit goes in a different direction than I want. I have to let it be the master and just follow where it leads."

"Will Jerry come for a visit soon?" America felt rather foolish asking the question because she was not sure she believed Aunt Dicy's explanations, but she yearned for an answer whether accurate or not.

"I do not know, child." Aunt Dicy knew America was impatient to know. "This answer was general and gentle in nature, as most usually are. So we will need to plan together. But, to be safe, you should wear a stalk of mugwort in your hair as a protection against evil. Some of our dispirited workers might get ideas of overpowering you."

"Will Mistress Rebecca object if I put an herb in my hair?"

"If you keep the mugwort hidden under your kerchief, no one is to know except you and me."

Chapter 20
Encouragement

AMERICA SETTLED INTO THE RHYTHM OF LIFE at Pleasant Green Hill Farm, making friends with Rose and Nina and learning what Mistress Rebecca expected of her. Henry was not a source of fright, but she remained on guard when he was near. She wore mugwort leaves under her kerchief. It gave her a sense of security, even though she was not convinced of its protection. Her ninety-eight year-old cabinmate was becoming like a grandmother to her.

Harriet and Sarah were delightful to be around, as they treated America like an older sister rather than a servant. Even though they all knew America was hired to help their mother, the girls had not acquired the haughty demeanor of their urban counterparts. Sharing her interest in reading, America solidified Harriet's estimation of her, although time to share Joel Tanner Hart's poems had not presented itself.

One afternoon, Harriet pulled out the blue beribboned packet. "Here is a poem Cousin Joel sent to Diana. She copied it down for me." As Harriet began to unfold the thick pages, she noticed America's confused look. "Diana is my age, one of my cousins on Father's side. She is the daughter of Joel's sister Mary."

"Miss Harriet, I do not know if I can make out the handwriting. If I have an idea of what is said, then I usually can pick out the words. Would you read it as I look at the writing?" America's eagerness to read fought with her caution of misunderstanding what she read.

"Yes. I like reading this poem aloud." Harriet began: "When Spring returned to mate the dove/ One morn, and wak'd the birds and bees,/Sister and I, with children's love/And play, set out two little trees.

"Winter-abashed in tawny white/and tattered, slid into the rills/While Flora scattered daisies bright/And violets, and daffodils.

"The chirp, the tap, the pheasant's drum/ Awoke the sleeping woods, and sweet/The breath of morn, the stir, the hum/Of tiny wing, and busy feet.

"The South's first herald, thistle down/Came gaily sailing on the breeze/The ants began their little town,/And moles plough'd round our tiny trees.

"We built our play-house when the thrush/ And jay made nests in tangled vine/Of bark, and moss, 'mid fern and brush/And named our nurslings, Mine and thine."

"Beautiful, Miss Harriet," America sighed. "Mine and thine." She thought of Jerry and of the possibilities Aunt Dicy predicted. But then she brought herself back to the present and said, "I can almost see the springtime in his poem."

"The title is 'Two Little Trees.' There are five more pages of it." Harriet folded the papers, as if to save the rest of the poem for another day.

America, although she knew she had other household duties, pressed her luck. "Miss Harriet, would you read that first page again? I would like to cast it in memory so I could pick out the words the next time."

"Why, yes, I would be happy to." She unfolded the paper. This time Harriet read more deliberately and pointed to the words as she said them.

"Thank you." America mused, "Mister Joel writes the same masterly way he works in plaster and stone. His work is so real. Your imagination is only left to admire how he does it. There is no mistaking his words or his art." She stopped talking. She had spoken too much.

"You are right, America. And, we can finish the poem another time." Harriet realized that America was not only respectful, she displayed great intelligence.

Each day, America looked for signs that her papa had come to the farm on a business visit. In her mind, she had rehearsed what she would say about Jerry. Not wanting to alarm him about Henry's interest, she sought to ask for help clearing the way to allow Jerry to visit. America thought Aunt Dicy's idea was good: letting Henry understand that Jerry's interest would serve to thwart any torment he might have in mind.

The next Tuesday, as America helped Rose and Nina prepare the dinner meal, she heard the trot and crunch of a horse and carriage advancing up the sycamore shaded lane. Through the kitchen window, she spied Henry appearing from the barn to take charge of the dust-begrimed horse. The driver had stepped down and walked into the barn. Henry immediately unhitched the driving tack and led the horse to the water trough in the shade. After tethering the horse, he turned to see after the dust-covered brougham.

"Oh, another mouth to feed for dinner!" Rose stopped stirring the pot of green beans and ham. She found a ceramic pitcher in the nearby cupboard. "America, go to the springhouse and fill this pitcher with cool water from the crock there. And bring in one of the lemons from the tree. I can make a lemon-honey shrub for Master and Mistress and the visitor."

"Yes, Rose." America was glad for the excuse to take a good look at the visitor. *Was it Papa? Had he come to see about me?*

She saw the brougham and almost dropped the earthenware pitcher. *Oh, no! McMillen the slave catcher! He went to Maysville! Has he come here to kidnap me?* America hid behind the shade tree near the water trough. She had to catch her breath. *That is his carriage. Oh, I am going to be sick!* As she clutched her stomach, Aunt Dicy stepped behind her.

"Girl, control yourself. The man is in the barn." The elderly slave's presence brought some comfort. America let out a whoop of relief. *That slave catcher will not try to kidnap me with Aunt Dicy and Henry around.*

"It is his carriage. The man who tried to kidnap me. I would know that brougham anywhere! He locked me in it last spring!" America had to stop and breathe. "It is horrible inside. Dark. Stinking. I was trapped just like all those other slaves."

"America, you are safe here." Aunt Dicy knew the right things to say.

"The curtains hid the shackles and the chamber pot." America shuddered at the memory.

Aunt Dicy stood on tiptoes and stretched to view the carriage. "The curtains are pulled back. I cannot see any shackles. Henry has unhitched the horse from the carriage. It cannot go anywhere. You are safe."

America remained behind the tree. "He lies. He told Uncle Eli that I was his girl and he was going to take me home! He might be saying anything to get me away!"

"Now, girl. Your master hired you out to Master Branch. Nobody will take you away if Master Branch has anything to do with it." Aunt Dicy tried to be reasonable.

"Papa." America tried to follow Aunt Dicy's calmness. "I sure wish he..." Suddenly, she remembered. "Oh, Aunt Dicy. I have been so foolish. Papa *is* here! That is his horse." America pointed. "That is his carriage." She pointed again.

"What? You said you had been locked in it by a slave catcher!"

Henry walked over to the two women, listening to the excitement of their words.

"I was." America held up her hands.

"Is your papa a slave catcher? Did he kidnap you?" Aunt Dicy was clearly confused, as was Henry.

America had to explain, but she also had to get the water and the lemons. "No. My papa is Master Murphy. He owns me. He is not a slave catcher. I *am* safe! I will tell you about it after dinner." She said this over her shoulder as she opened the door to the springhouse, slipping into the dark coolness of the small enclosure. Physical movement brought relief: it wiped away all the terror of the past moments. America cleared her mind in the welcome coolness of the small stone outbuilding.

Willie rang the bronze dinner bell, and Nina and America brought the bowls and platters to the dining table as Rose finished frying the potato cakes. Just as Rose delivered the savory pancakes to the table, the family entered the room with their visitor who had just been greeted by Master Branch. Aunt Dicy, keeping an eye on America, stayed in the kitchen to fill water glasses and to ready the dessert dishes. The meals had begun to take on a choreography of their own, as each servant efficiently did her part. Silently, when America brought a dish to the dining room, she smiled at her Master Murphy who gave her a wink.

At the end of the meal, after the pudding cups were cleared, the children were excused to go outside. Master and Mistress Tanner invited Jeremiah to sit on the porch to enjoy a lemon shrub, catch a breeze, and talk business. The servants tidied the dining room, washed and put away the dishes, and then ate their own dinner. Over the quick meal, America explained to Aunt Dicy, Rose, and

Nina an account of her kidnapping, escape, and the obvious fright it had produced.

"But how does your master own the horse and carriage?" Aunt Dicy wanted to know.

"He bought it at the sheriff's auction of Lewis Robards' possessions," America told them. "The slave catcher McMillen was using Lewis Robards' conveyance to transport slaves. Master Murphy bought that very set I was locked in. He said he would refinish and restore it to use in his livery business. 'You will not recognize it because it will be new inside and out when I am finished with it,' is what he told me. Well, he was wrong on that account." America just shook her head.

After a brief quiet pause, Aunt Dicy stood up. "Come along, America. This must be done before your master comes to the cabin to visit with you."

"What, Aunt Dicy?" America saw the determined look on the servant's face. Aunt Dicy led America toward the path to the quarters. When they got to the shade tree that America had hidden behind, she stopped. Aunt Dicy grabbed her hand.

"You must face your fears, America." She motioned with the jerk of her head toward the carriage that Jeremiah had driven. "You and I are going to sit in that coach."

"Why, Aunt Dicy?" America stood her ground. "I know what it once was. And how frightened it made me. We know that Master Murphy has cleaned and painted it and fixed it up. It is safe now. I know that."

"Your head knows that. Your body needs to be convinced." The ninety-eight year old slave held America's hand as they walked toward the carriage. Henry had taken the horse to the barn.

America bared her teeth as if to bite Aunt Dicy, just like she did with the kidnapper. She thought better of it and closed her mouth. Her fingers spread apart and she curved them into claws, ready to scratch Aunt Dicy. She thought better of it and relaxed. When Aunt Dicy opened the door of the brougham, the odor of the new varnish and upholstery fabric wafted to them in the heat of midday. America grabbed the door frame and pushed against Aunt Dicy.

"Girl, we are going to sit inside. Do not fight me. We will keep the doors open. You will see that it is safe."

"Aunt Dicy, I am going to be sick." America stepped back and gagged. The noonday meal burned a path around her middle, encircling her back and ribs.

"That is no excuse. This carriage is not your master. You stand up to its fearsome presence! It cannot ruin you. Only your memory of it can ruin you." Aunt Dicy was adamant.

"All right." America stepped into the carriage. "I am safe. I am safe. I know I am safe. This is strange." Then she remembered the chant she said to herself when she was kidnapped. Closing her eyes she repeated: "Well, well, Magic Spell, get me out of this prison cell. Well, well, Magic Spell, get me out of this prison cell." She opened and closed her fists in rhythm to her words. It worked. She relaxed and opened her eyes and smiled at Aunt Dicy.

"Girl, you did it." Aunt Dicy was satisfied. She got in and looked around at the rich fittings and smooth woodwork. "Fancy." Then she squeezed America's arm. "You faced this prison cell and won the body battle. Your spirit should be comfortable now."

Harriet, Sarah, and David appeared in the yard. "America, is this your master's carriage?"

"Yes, Miss Harriet," America smiled down at them.

"Is he going to take you away?" Sarah spoke up. America playing house with her a few days ago, had sewn a tiny apron for her favorite doll. The youngest Tanner daughter clutched the doll to her chest as if to ward off any departures. But she kept her thumb firmly in her mouth.

America spied David walking around the carriage, dwarfed by the size of it.

"No, Miss Sarah. Aunt Dicy and I were just inspecting this fine coach." America made room on the seat. "Would you like to come sit in it? We can pretend you are Cinderella on her way to the ball. Remember that story Miss Harriet read to us?" America nodded at the older sister.

"Oh, yes. We would be pleased to sit in this fine carriage." Harriet answered for the younger girl. She offered her hand to America, as she had seen done before, and boosted herself inside. Then she turned to leverage up Sarah, who had to jump up to the step to gain entry. David wandered into the barn to inspect the visiting horse. The coach became crowded with feminine talk and giggles. America was quite pleased with the outcome, which had been forced by Aunt Dicy's demands. She showed a happy, triumphant smile to the elderly, fellow slave.

Jeremiah appeared, interrupting the gaiety.

"Pa-Master Murphy!" America scrambled down from the carriage, as Aunt Dicy shepherded the young girls away.

"Do you approve of the changes I made to the carriage?" Jeremiah did not expect an answer. "I drove it over to test its strength and maneuverability. The horse needed some exercise, too. And, as I said I would, I came to see how you are doing. The Tanners are pleased so far."

"And, I too, am pleased to be here. But," she hesitated. Determined to get to the point, America began her explanation. "Could you speak to the Tanners about giving permission for Jerry to come visit? I know they have to approve, but, as my owner, your good word carries a lot of weight in such a decision."

"Jerry is hired out to his owner's cousin in Bourbon County." Jeremiah wanted to understand the logistics of the proposal.

"Yes. But part of his duties is to see after the horses and to drive the wagon and carriage for Master John Skillman. He could come here with one of the horses. My guess is that Master Skillman would allow him to do that. His work is similar to what Henry does here." America indicated the barn area with a nod of her head, though her face hardened a bit.

"I will speak to Master Tanner about Jerry. Master Skillman in Bourbon County would have to agree to allow Jerry to come for Sunday visits." Jeremiah cleared his throat. "Has anyone here shown an interest in you as a beau?"

"No one to take Jerry's place." America looked at the dirt swirling around her feet. A slight breeze had disturbed the air. "Jerry is so kind, resourceful, and handsome. And, he can read!"

"I know." Jeremiah looked around. "I would like to see your quarters. Your mama wants to know."

"I want you to meet Aunt Dicy. She and I are cabinmates and share all sorts of secrets." America chuckled as she led him to the cabin. "She just helped me get over the fright of seeing that carriage again. I *did* recognize it even though you have refinished it from top to bottom."

"Merry, Merry, not contrary. How was one to know?" Papa tried to defend himself in a comforting way, beginning the call and response.

"Hmmm. With wishing wells and fears that swell and nightmares all in a row." America had an answer, even if it was nonsense. "I feel safe here, but that brougham brought back too many painful memories. It made me sick, but now I am fully recovered. I expect the horse is happier, too."

"Yes. Sometimes our minds accept things that our hearts cannot let go of." Jeremiah studied the cabin and the open door hung with netting.

"Before we go in, come take a look at the garden Aunt Dicy keeps in the back. It is full of herbs and medicine plants, some that have survived the drought and some that are just drying in the sunshine." America stepped between the first and second row of the plants. "Here. Please take some of this thyme to Mama. With my love. And Aunt Dicy's regards." She wanted to show Jeremiah and Anne, especially, that, so far, she was secure and happy with her life at Pleasant Green Hill. "Now, let us get in from the sun."

Jeremiah walked through the door as America held the netting back. He looked around, his eyes adjusting to the cooler, darkened room. Aunt Dicy had returned from the big house and was sitting in her rocking chair near the window opening in the far wall, mending an apron in the light of a sunbeam. The room looked cozy and cheery despite the lack of light. The cool mud floor and the idle fireplace helped to lower the temperature, like a dry cave lined with rough-cut wood. It welcomed Jeremiah, just like Anne's kitchen at home. He instinctively took off his hat.

"Merry, Merry, not contrary, how does your garden grow?" With a smile, he waited for America's response.

"With silver bells," America paused. *The silver hand bells Mistress Henrietta and Mistress Rebecca ring at the dinner table. And Willie rang the old bronze farm bell.*

"And magic spells," she paused again. *The magic chant I made up when I was kidnapped-it seemed to work! And, Aunt Dicy's mugwort spell.*

"And bright colors all in a row." *Jerry's quilt squares are going to be in a row!*

A smile brightened her face, reflecting the delight in Papa's eyes. "With silver bells and magic spells and bright colors all in a row!" America sang it the second time. "Heavens, Papa! Those words have been my life this past year. How did that happen?"

"More than that happened this year."

"A lot has changed," America admitted, shaking her head. "Master Murphy, here is Aunt Dicy. She has helped me get used to this farm." America led Jeremiah over to the elder slave who had risen from her chair and stood straight at attention.

"Dicy, it is encouraging to know that you are here: it is a good sign that the Tanners keep you on." Jeremiah voiced the positive statement as much for America's benefit as for Aunt Dicy's.

"Well, sir, I try to do as much as I can." Aunt Dicy accepted his statement as a compliment. "America is a smart, willing worker. She takes the place of granddaughters I wish I knew."

"And, you, Aunt Dicy, take the place of the grandmothers I do not know." *One white grandmother and one black grandmother.* America smiled at her cabinmate and gave her arm a squeeze.

Jeremiah took a final look around the cabin before stepping back through the door. "The year is not over, America. There might be more changes to come." He put his derby hat back on. "I will speak to the Tanners about Jerry coming to see you."

"Thank you, Papa," America whispered to him as she realized how fortunate she was. "Please give my love to Mama, along with the thyme, of course. Please tell her that I am happy to be here."

Chapter 21
Hope

JEREMIAH'S HORSE AND BUGGY APPEARED in the Tanner yard the third Tuesday in October. The steady rain that came two days before had broken the fragile dryness of the long summer drought; however it was not enough to help the field crops. The prospect of normal fall temperatures was encouraging, but the cloud-filled skies reflected a gloomy mood.

As soon as Henry met the conveyance, America could tell that Jeremiah's visit was to be short. Master Murphy alighted from the small carriage and gave instructions to the slave. Henry led the horse to the water trough, but kept him hitched up.

From the set of his shoulders and attention to details, America's master looked as if he had more than one purpose to accomplish with this visit. America watched him make his way to the small study that served as Branch Tanner's office.

Having reached a financial agreement with Master Tanner concerning feed and hay for his livery stable, Jeremiah hastened to seek out America. He made his way to the kitchen where America was scrubbing the pots from the breakfast meal. She immediately went to his side.

"Master Murphy, this is Rose." America gestured as she introduced them.

Rose, stirring the batter for the next meal's dessert, stopped her work, and addressed Jeremiah with a subservient nod. "Pleased to meet you."

"America will show me her quarters. We will not be long." Jeremiah displayed his authority.

America nodded to Rose and smiled at Jeremiah. As they left the kitchen, America had to find out. "Papa, have you any news about Jerry?" She asked the question softly, so as not to be overheard, but was almost afraid to hear the answer.

"Merry, I have news. Most of it is good, but there is some sad news." Jeremiah studied her face. "Here is the sad news first. Then I will leave after I tell you the happy news because I should be on my way shortly." He paused, controlling a sigh. "Reverend London Ferrill died unexpectedly last week. Heart trouble. I am sorry he passed away because, you know, he was a good friend."

America came to a stop. "Oh, Papa! He was a good friend. He told some amusing stories when he came to our house."

As they continued their stroll to the cabin, Jeremiah resumed his explanation. "Many people in Lexington held him in high regard, and the funeral procession was long. Some thought it was the biggest one since Henry Clay's funeral two years ago. Mourners of both races came to pay respect. That is saying a lot for a colored man, you know. The newspaper said there were seventy carriages and sixty people on horseback with about four thousand people at the grave site."

"Papa. Did you take part in it?" America asked. "Did Mama sew an armband for you?"

"Yes. She saw to it that I wore appropriate attire. I was so busy with my livery horses and carriages for the mourners, I did not join the procession through town."

"Well, Lexington lost a good man-a free man of color." America could feel Jeremiah's sadness.

"That is true. We all benefitted from being around him." The door to the cabin was opened wide, and the netting was gone along with the heat of the past days. Jeremiah refused to continue the conversation about his good friend. Instead, he greeted America's cabinmate, "Aah, Aunt Dicy."

The elder slave hesitated sweeping the hard-packed dirt floor of the cabin and looked up to him in surprise. "Good day to you, Master Murphy. Will you have a seat?"

"I will not be long." He did not remove his hat but stood a few steps inside the door. Turning to America he said, "Now, I have good news. I decided to see if there was support from Master Abraham Skillman for Jerry's visits. The Tanners had already approved."

"Yes?" America could not hide her interest. Aunt Dicy, storing the broom away, listened closely but did not enter the conversation.

"Master Abraham said he would take up the matter on his next trip to visit his cousin." Papa paused to tease America. "I just happened to see him yesterday, standing on the street paying his respects as Reverend Ferrill's funeral passed by."

"Yes, Papa?" America repeated quietly, waiting for the happy news.

"He told me that it was all right with him and Master John Skillman for Jerry to come here on Sundays. The hemp processing is in full swing now, but Sunday is a day of rest from labor."

"Oh, that is the best good news!" America clapped her hands, showing how pleased she was.

"Master Abraham Skillman said that when he saw Jerry for that short time, he hinted that visiting here might be possible." Jeremiah's eyes twinkled. "I wonder who Jerry might be interested in seeing."

"Now, Master," America eyes twinkled back. "Maybe he will come to see if the book collection is adequate for the Tanner family, or if Master Tanner needs help fixing a wagon, or if Master Tanner..."

"And you will just happen to be here to greet him," Jeremiah interrupted playing along.

"Why, yes. What a pleasant happenstance! No contrariness on my part." America laughed at the thought, as did her papa.

"Merry, I just remembered." His face wreathed a smile. "I have a package for you. In the carriage. Come with me to get it. Then I will be on my way."

"Something Mama sent?" America could only guess.

"No, it is from Aunt Bette by way of Cook and Uncle Eli." Jeremiah added to her anticipation as they quickly walked to the horse and buggy that Henry secured near the barn.

"Here it is." He handed over a paper-wrapped parcel.

America took the package and then sat on the carriage block to unwrap it in her lap. "Oh, Papa!" She recognized paper that had been saved in the Hopemont pantry for wrapping items. "Did you see what this is?"

"Yes, Merry. Uncle Eli said that Mistress Henrietta was cleaning out the children's bedroom with Aunt Bette. When they came upon this book without a cover, Aunt Bette remembered your first introduction to Jerry. You called a book's cover, a blanket." He smiled. "Since Thomas and Key had grown away from such books, Mistress Henrietta decided to get rid of it in its poor condition. Aunt Bette offered to send it to you. So, here it is."

"She must have given it to Cook, who gave it to Uncle Eli, who gave it to you." America guessed how the bound pages wrapped in paper came to her. She looked at the title page: *The Only True Mother Goose Melodies.* "Papa, I know all the words in the title except the last one. What is it?"

"Melodies." He pronounced the word slowly and softly. "Melodies. Like songs. But what the pages contain are nursery rhymes."

"Miss Catherine read some nursery rhymes to me. It will be amusing to read and share with Harriet and Sarah, and with Jerry when he comes!" The idea that he would be visiting her was never far from her mind. "But of most importance is that I now have a book of my own! Thank you for bringing it to me. And would you please say thank you to Uncle Eli? Maybe he could pass on my greetings and thanks to Cook and Aunt Bette. I feel so lucky to know them."

"Before I go, Mistress Merry, turn to page eighty-nine." Jeremiah's eyes were twinkling again.

"Eight, nine." America was very careful. "Here it is."

"Look at the poem on the bottom of the page," Jeremiah directed her.

"All right." America pointed to the beginning words. "Mistress Mary, quite contrary. Oh, Papa! It is the real nursery rhyme you taught me!"

"Our rhyme is real, Merry," Papa answered. "Even though you are not a mistress and you are not contrary. Go on and read those words. They are what Mother taught me."

"How does your garden grow?/With silver bells and cockle shells/And maidens all in a row." America looked up. "Huh. I like our version much better. Merry, Merry, not contrary, how does your garden grow? With silver bells, and magic spells, and bright colors all in a row."

"That fits us, pretty much. I hope you will always have silver bells and magic spells and bright colors." He turned to climb into the buggy.

"I hope color will become a good thing-not a means to judge people. Thank you, Papa, for this wonderful gift. It gives me courage to continue to get better." America gave him a squeeze on his arm.

"Your mama and I were speaking about you recently." He paused as he gathered up the reins. "She said that you possess the courage. No, what was her word? The *audacity* to hope for a better life."

"Well, Papa, I guess I do. I am always looking to improve myself. Please give my love to Mama."

"Yes. Goodbye. And say hello to Jerry for me!" Jeremiah directed his words over his shoulder as the pull of the horse started his journey back to Lexington.

"Fare thee well, Master. Thank you!" America turned to resume her work in the Tanner kitchen and to her life as a servant in that household.

Chapter 22
Jerry visits

IT WAS SUNDAY. AMERICA HAD SEEN after the children, helping them into their Sunday-best clothes. The Branch Tanner family had since departed for the weekly church service a few miles away. Rose and Nina accompanied them but sat in the segregated pews for black attendees.

Would Jerry be coming today?

"Child, looking out the window every fifteen minutes will not bring him any sooner." Aunt Dicy nodded at the kitchen window that faced the stable yard. The mantle clock had just chimed the quarter hour as the two women settled to their mending chores in front of the fireplace. The elderly slave checked the liquid in the large Dutch oven that hung over the glowing logs: the beef roast inside it was simmering in the seasoned juices. The heat from the fire served to make the spacious room cozy.

Except for the size, this is just as comfortable as the kitchen at home. But, when everybody is working in here, it is busy and crowded – not a suitable place to visit with Jerry. Where can we go? Maybe the barn. It should be warm with the heat from the horses and the shelter of the hay and straw stored there.

"We will need more firewood if that roast is to be ready for dinner when the folks get home." Aunt Dicy inspected the depleted fuel supply next to the cooking area. "Henry always has a stack ready. Go get some before things get busy here."

America was glad to go out. *I will see about the stable area. That is where Jerry would bring the horse anyhow. It will be an excuse to show Henry that I have a protector who will be coming regularly.*

Bending over the stack of firewood near the barn, America loaded the pieces into her apron skirt, choosing just the right size for the kitchen fireplace. *I wonder how Jerry will get here. Will he use the roads, or come cross country, or follow the waterways?*

She felt a tap on her shoulder. "Jerry! I did not think…" Turning around, her smile vanished. The fuel logs fell from her apron.

Henry.

"Ah. You did not think." Henry put his hands on his hips and tilted his head to one side. "Here I caught you doing honest labor and not thinking. That is against what you said when I first met you."

"I do a lot of hard work-cleaning, washing, ironing, scrubbing. But, we need not be considered work animals like livestock! We have minds capable of any thinking that would come our way." America stooped to pick up the pieces of wood and put them in the sling of her apron again. Henry folded his arms, watching her.

"Well, pretty one. You look lively to me! 'Live-stock!' But if thinking is on your mind, I'll give you something to think on. The family is gone right now, along with Rose and Nina and Willie. The field hands have their own church doings in the woods. What say you come into the stable with me, and we can have our own doings."

America stood up and faced him with a scowl. "Never. I will call Aunt Dicy if need be. You put one hand on me, I will scream for her."

"A lot of good that will do." He paused. "She is old." He looked America up and down. "You are young-and fresh-if manners are considered. I can teach you a thing or two about how to get along." He reached for her, daring her to scream.

America obliged. Jerking away from his reach, she yelled for Aunt Dicy. Her voice reverberated off the buildings in the still Sunday morning quiet. Even though it did not send an alarm to Aunt Dicy, it was enough to stop Henry's advances.

"I have a friend," her voice trembled before she swallowed and squared her shoulders.

"Ah, that must be who you took me for a minute ago," Henry interrupted, and, trying to be sociable, folded his arms again.

"Yes. Jerry is his name. He will be coming to visit me." She halfway relaxed when Henry stopped his teasing behavior.

"Today?" Henry wanted to find out as much as he could. "He must be a worker at another farm."

"Yes. When he gets here, I would like you to meet him." America softened her demeanor. She knew that if she and Jerry were to visit uninterrupted in the stable or anywhere else on the farm, she would need Henry's kindness and cooperation and respect.

"I would like to be friends with another black man." Henry took a friendly stance. "Beside the hired field hands, I have only Willie to talk with." Henry defined an attitude that America had not considered before: he wanted the companionship of fellow bondsmen.

"I can see that. We learn a lot from fellow workers." America had learned her duties from older, more experienced female slaves, including her mama. She now understood that Henry did not have any friendships or support from black male workers. *Maybe that is why he has been such a threat and a tease. I guess I will find out if Jerry and Henry can be distant friends and in turn be a protection for me. I wish Jerry would appear!*

Later that day, after the noon meal had been served, the dining room put to order, and the kitchen cleaned to Rose's satisfaction, America spent time with Harriet and Sarah, hemming dish towels. She cut the linen crash fabric to the desired length, and then pinned the folded ends in place. Sarah, who was just mastering the use of needle and thread, ran basting stitches along the hem. Finally, Harriet would take her turn running a fine line of whip stitches to secure the hem producing a useful, sturdy kitchen towel.

Just as the sisters gathered up the sewing materials, preparing for their Sunday afternoon reading and writing activities, America heard the clopping of a single horse entering the stable yard. She had been listening for that sound all day.

Jerry had arrived.

Reuben, David, and Willie were playing with their slingshots in the stable yard. As soon as they noticed Jerry riding towards them, they all stopped to determine what should be done. Jerry communicated to the farm horse to slow down and then pulled on the reins to stop its forward motion. The horse willingly paused. Eight-year-old Willie ran into the stable as ten-year-old Reuben and five-year-old David stood their ground, acting, for all to see, as the farm's proprietors. Jerry slid down from the saddle and, keeping a tight hold of the reins on the tired horse, tipped his hat to the two white boys.

"Good afternoon. Is this the home of Master Branch Tanner?" Jerry was respectful to the brothers as if they were the masters of the farm.

"Yes. What is your business here?" Reuben did not mince words.

"I am Jerry from Willow Valley Farm. My master is John Skillman." Jerry placed the reins firmly under one arm as he opened the rough fabric pouch slung across his chest. "I have a letter of permission written by my master for Master Branch Tanner."

Henry and Willie appeared at that moment. "Are you Jerry?" Henry took charge, giving the impression of an overseer.

Surprised, Jerry answered immediately. "This letter of permission is for Master Tanner from my master, John Skillman."

Henry took the paper as if to read, having no idea what it said. Reuben held out his hand for it and then motioned to Jerry to follow him to his father's office. Jerry handed the reins to Henry, and then took his hat off, wiped his face on his sleeve, and looked around the yard as he kept up with the young Tanner boys.

It was not long before Jerry returned to the stable yard. He untethered the Skillman horse that Henry had secured to the hitching post and led it to the water trough near the now bare shade tree.

America had watched from the kitchen window as she put away the sewing materials. She hurried outside. "Hello, Jerry." The smile on her face indicated her happiness to see him.

"Good afternoon, America." Jerry's grin displayed his relief that he had found the right place, coupled with the understanding that America welcomed his presence. The horse raised its head from the trough, and Jerry handed the reins to America. He went about inspecting and unsaddling the animal. Taking the reins back in one hand, he carried the saddle on the other arm, and led the horse to the barn. "I will meet you here as soon as I see about the horse."

America walked to the slave cabin and emerged shortly, holding her paper-covered nursery-rhyme book now bound with a leather strap. She sat on the wooden bench outside her quarters to wait for Jerry to tend to the horse. Both hired servants were aware that they were being watched.

"Hello, Merry Murphy," Jerry murmured as he sat down on the bench.

"Hello, Jerry Burns," America replied, letting her sparkling eyes speak her welcome. "I am glad Master John allowed the use of his horse. Did you have trouble finding the way here?"

"Mister Crocket, the teacher who is staying at the farm, had an idea of this location. He told me to stay within sight of the creek beds to get here. Because of the drought, there was not much water in the creeks, but the rock beds are evident. I first had to find the wide bed of Stoner Creek near the many toll pikes in Bourbon County, then we walked south following the direction of the creek until I spotted the little creek bed that connected into the bigger creek. It led us here. Well, almost. I had to ask a group of black men who were walking back from their church meeting in the woods. They told me how to find Master Branch's house."

Henry suddenly appeared, giving America a start-again. However, she immediately remembered her manners. "Jerry, this is Henry."

"Henry. We met, but I did not know your name. Now I do." Jerry seemed to invite more conversation.

Still tense around Henry, America tried to smooth things along. "If I understand from the letter you wrote me, Henry's responsibilities are similar to yours, Jerry."

"I take care of the horses and conveyances, see after the livestock, and do errands for the master and mistress." Henry smiled proudly and gestured with his right hand toward the spacious barn. "Master Branch and Mistress Rebecca count on me to keep things in order."

"Yes, I can see that." Jerry looked around appreciatively. "That is about what I do, too, besides working in the fields. And are you training the boy to help with your work?"

"His name is Willie. My son." Henry cleared his throat, then went on. "His mama was owned by Master Ecton, not far from here. Willie is good help for his age."

"What happened to his mama?" America had to ask.

"She was sold away about this time last year, so the master could buy more men to work his fields." Henry shrugged his shoulders and looked from America to Jerry. "Master Branch bought me and Willie at the same time. He is here with me, and can learn what I do. I hope he will be good enough so he won't be sent to the fields."

"Yes." America hoped that her position was safe, too, but knew she was dependent on her papa's business savvy. *Jerry's status is more questionable! Well, I will just enjoy his company as long as I can and maybe add to his happiness.* She looked at the nursery-rhyme book in her lap. "And speaking of learning, I own a book now. It is from Aunt Bette, by way of Master Murphy. Take a look, Jerry." The leather strap kept the loose pages together.

"Can you read? And write?" Henry jumped into the conversation despite good manners not to. He addressed Jerry, ignoring America.

"Yes. I can." Jerry squinted at Henry, wondering where the talk was going to lead and if he would be able to converse with America alone. He unwound the worn leather band and unfolded the paper cover, preparing to read the beginning pages.

"You can read the papers for news about slave sales and runaways and about what the whites are planning to do." Henry's statement was punctuated with looks to the right and left, checking for eavesdrops. He lowered his voice so that only Jerry could hear, "You could write out a pass if you needed."

"But I will not." Jerry was firm in his answer. He stopped, then added to his resolve. "Henry, I came all this way to see America. I followed the rules about permission to travel." He patted the fabric pouch hanging across his chest. "I am protecting this pass that Master Skillman wrote and Master Tanner and Master Murphy approved. I will not ruin the trust they have placed in me and America."

Henry persisted with his questions. "If you could lay hands on a newspaper that had stories about abolitionists like Cassius Clay or Delia Webster, would you read it aloud in your quarters?"

"I would read a paper if I could get hold of one." Jerry was getting restive.

"Would you let on if you knew someone was going to be sold down the river?" Henry pressed the subject.

"Yes. And I am sure you would too." Jerry studied Henry's face. He absently wound the leather strip around his right hand.

"If only I had known ahead of time." Henry shook his head, his face taking on a melancholy look. "I know now that I must check all possibilities. We cannot know our chances unless we provoke an exchange." He almost apologized for questioning Jerry.

In spite of her desire to visit with Jerry, America understood Henry's overbearing behavior: he sought the company of a fellow male slave, someone who would see his point of view. She almost felt sorry for him.

Jerry's feelings were couched in distrust. *Henry's questions border on unlawful conduct. He could be a threat. Would he try to woo America to take the place of Willie's mama? Or would he abuse America as a show of masterful strength?* Whatever the cause, Jerry decided to show Henry his own strength and fortitude.

"Well, Henry, I want to be very clear about my interests today and for the future. I came to visit with America and plan to come every Sunday. I know that America's Master Murphy looks kindly on that arrangement. He will be journeying over, when need be, to see after his business with Master Tanner. If I find anything amiss with regard to America, you can be sure that I will fashion a note to him. In the meantime, you can count on my ability to take things into my own hands." He studied the leather strap covering his knuckles and, unwinding the leather, he punctuated his words with a smacking leather whack against his own leg. "I know ways to make things difficult for you *and* for Willie."

"It is Willie's future that I am thinking of." Henry raised his voice as a protest to Jerry's threat. "If he knew how to read, things would be better for us."

"We all wonder about the future, Henry." Jerry did not back down from what he guessed was a diversion from possible unlawful activities.

"Willie is smart for his age. He catches on to things quickly." Henry was clearly proud of his son but was concerned that Willie would be a slave for life. "How did you learn to read?"

"My master in Lexington taught me, to help with his book trade. He needed someone to unload the shipped parcels, organize orders, and tend to requests." Jerry's face reflected sadness. He knew he would never return to that life.

"Willie has no prospects that way. The only touch he has with book learning is when Reuben brings out his toy soldiers. The young master keeps a folded newspaper with the set and reads on it to set up the lines of battle with the toy soldiers. Willie plays along with him but has to follow Reuben's instructions, which he gets from that old paper. I have seen them play Mexican War battles because that is what the paper tells. They know who wins, but it is like the boys and toy soldiers are being ordered around by what is printed on the paper."

"Reading makes a difference." America advised him.

"Have you been able to get any book learning from the girls?" Henry knew that America spent more time with Harriet and Sarah. "I know they play school."

"We have shared some poems and rhymes." America looked down at her hands. "I have worked more on sewing skills when I am with them. Most of my time has been helping Rose and Nina with cooking, cleaning, and laundry." She looked at Jerry with a wistful expression. "I was hoping you would help me with the printed word."

Jerry's face matched her woebegone look. Then he struck his left hand with the leather strap as if he had an inspiration. "I just had a thought. Maybe we can do something about the schooling. You know how a young horse will be more obliging to follow if an older one leads the way?" He looked at Henry.

"Yes." Neither Henry nor America could see what he was getting at.

"Well, America is the older horse in terms of reading. Willie is the younger, more inexperienced colt."

"Jerry, I have no time to teach him the little that I know. Besides, I do not think he would be willing to learn from me." *Willie would just follow Henry's teasing behavior.*

"Oh, he will be willing. I will see to that." Henry was firm with that statement, acting as the head of his own household. "He has no choice in the matter. I want him to be knowledgeable."

"I have a better idea, an arrangement that should work for everyone." Jerry showed his diplomatic side. "On Sundays, when I call on America, I will share reading with both America and Willie. We will meet in the barn. We have America's nursery-rhyme book, and I will bring a Bible and maybe borrow a schoolbook from Mister Crocket."

"Oh, Jerry. That sounds great!" America clapped her hands once, to show her pride and admiration.

"Of course, I will not spend all my time with Willie. I plan to have most of America's undivided attention during my Sunday sojourn."

"Sounds good to me. I will see about fixing a suitable empty stall." Henry suddenly became aware of someone standing quietly near the corner of the cabin. Willie. "Ah, come here, son."

When Willie shuffled over, he bobbed his head at Jerry. "I know some letters."

"Hello, Willie," America answered him. *He is brash just like his papa.* "What letters do you know?"

"I know that my name begins with a *W*. It looks like peaks and valleys. And Papa's name begins with an *H*. It looks like a rail fence. I can make those letters in the dirt. That's how Reuben taught me."

"It looks like you are ready for more schooling!" America was encouraged. *It will be fun to share words and letters with him the way Catherine taught me, even if it does take away from my Sunday time with Jerry.* She took the leather strap from Jerry's hands and quickly wrapped it around the nursery-rhyme book. She hoped it was a signal to Henry and Willie that their conversation with Jerry was over for the day. She wanted to introduce him to Aunt Dicy.

But Jerry seemingly wanted to continue the talk with the boy and his papa. He motioned for America to wait for him on the bench. The three males walked to the barn together. As she was waiting, America peeked into the glass kitchen window, searching for Aunt Dicy. She noticed that Rose and Nina were tiptoeing around a dozing figure. In the cozy heat of the kitchen, Aunt Dicy had given in to a restorative snooze, her mending items in her lap.

"Is the barn a suitable place for our reading time?" America asked when Jerry returned. She was curious about his conversation, but did not wish to pry. "It seems that Henry keeps everything clean and organized."

"Yes. I think it will do." Jerry answered her, and then decided to explain the reason for his private talk with

Henry. "I had a word with him about his conduct around you and how he could show his appreciation for the lessons we will be giving Willie. We came to an understanding. He will show the respect that is due to you. And he agreed to be your protector from any male slave that might want to harm you."

"Oh, Mister Jerry Burns. You are my hero, as well as a mind reader. How could you tell that Henry was an aggravation to me?"

"One look at you would lead any man to thoughts of conquest." Jerry gazed at her with a protective look. "I knew that Henry had rankled you somehow, by your uneasiness in his presence. I wanted to put my foot down before his advances got out of hand."

"Thank you, Jerry." Already, Jerry's visit had put America's mind at rest. "I want you to meet Aunt Dicy. Please come in the kitchen."

The opening and closing of the back door roused Aunt Dicy from her snooze. She sat up straight and looked around at the smiling Rose and Nina, and then, America and Jerry. "You caught me. I was having a beautifully soft dream."

"Aunt Dicy and Rose and Nina," America got their attention. "I want you to meet Jerry. He will be coming over every Sunday afternoon, we hope."

"Jerry." Aunt Dicy looked him up and down as if inspecting a fine racehorse. Although her inspection did not lead to laying hands on him, her smile indicated her approval. If she had money to buy a horse and he was up for auction, everyone knew she would bid on him. "My dream had doings in it that involved you."

"Tell us about it, Aunt Dicy." America made the request. Jerry put on a patient face.

"Well, maybe the ticking of the clock must have led me into the dream. What I remember is that time passes-years. You and Jerry are still seeing each other, and your

162

friendship has deepened into love. A broom appears, and it is placed on the floor between two people. Someone says 'til death or distance part." She paused and smiled, knowing that everyone knew how the phrase was used. "Then numbers came to me: a one and then an eight, then six, and then another one. 1-8-6-1. A year? Whatever it is, that number is very important because I saw a two-faced head. Whenever I see that in a dream, it means that I need to think about what else was shown to me. Maybe 1861 is a message. That year will not come for a while. But it seems as if it is important to both you and to me."

Rose and Nina had heard of Aunt Dicy's dreams but never had known them to be as real as this one seemed. They, along with America, had considered them as harmless-like dew sparkling in the morning light or a rainbow. It could be that Jerry's presence lent an air of substance that made Aunt Dicy explain her snoozing vision with more realism.

"My goodness, Aunt Dicy. You have given my imagination some wings." Then America remembered what was important to tell her cabinmate. "I wanted to tell you that Jerry met Henry and Willie." She looked at Jerry.

"Yes." Jerry nodded. "We have come to know each other, and I think we might even become friends. I plan to journey over here each week."

"I see that you are on the right path toward taking care of things, and America will welcome your visit." Aunt Dicy spoke as if America was her granddaughter.

"I am glad to meet you all." He included everyone with his look around the room. "I must bid you goodbye. Now that I know how to get here, I need to estimate how long my journey takes in preparation for next Sunday's visit. Timing is important. Once we are fairly close to Willow Valley farm, Master Skillman's horse will get us back to the comfort of his own stable in no time."

"I will walk with you to the barn, Jerry." America regretted the day's short visit but knew that longer conversations would take place in the future.

After Jerry saddled the farm horse and climbed on its back, he leaned down to plant a quick kiss on America's upturned face. "Goodbye, Merry Murphy. I expect to scatter a few more kisses the next time I come."

"Goodbye, Jerry Burns." America replied, touching her forehead. "Please remember to ask Mr. Crocket about a lesson book to borrow."

"I will remember." Jerry waved his hat as he urged the horse forward. "And I will see about borrowing a Bible, too."

"Fare thee well, Jerry!"

Chapter 23
Christmas

THE TANNER HOUSEHOLD started Christmas preparations in November. America was occupied with sewing work, as was Mistress Rebecca and the girls. Because of the drought, Master Branch Tanner had not hired a gang of hemp laborers that year, but he did rent a small group of slaves for farm tasks and to labor in the meager hemp harvest. The slaves' master had written in the contract that each of his bondsmen be provided a new set of clothes at the end of their contracted labor, which was December 25. America's responsibility was sewing those garments for the field hands. Grateful that she had to make clothing sets for just five hired slaves, she took on the task of sewing clothing for Henry and Willie, too. The clothes had to be finished by Christmas.

A packet containing bolts of blue striped osnaburg, Kentucky jean, gray brown linsey-woolsey, and brown Lowell cotton, along with thread, needles, and pins was shipped to the Tanner house from Shropshire & Cassell in Lexington. Its arrival signaled the beginning of the increased activity to get everything done before Christmas. The holiday marked a time when slaveholders gave new clothing and sometimes small gifts to their servants.

The mistress cut out the Kentucky jean and Lowell fabric to make as many pairs of pants possible for the slaves. She handed the scissors over to America to cut the other fabrics to make shirts for the male workers. At Christmas, each slave was to be given two pairs of sturdy workpants with three shirts that had to last them for a year. The leftover osnaburg and linsery-woolsey fabric was to be given to Aunt Dicy, Rose, and Nina.

No patterns were used, nor measurements taken to fit the fabric to the frame of the workers' bodies. The clothes were meant to be fairly loose to allow for strenuous movement, but snug enough to accommodate many cuttings from one bolt of fabric. Fashion or style was never considered. As the weeks passed, America carried out her assignment efficiently, although she worried about the clothes for eight-year-old Willie, who would be growing in height and weight in the next year.

House servants and children were obliged to scrub, shine, polish, and clean the whole house as Christmas guests were expected this year for dinner. Master Branch had taken on a leadership role in the extensive Tanner family. In order to show his capabilities as a senior member of the group, he wanted to present his well-run household as an example of his good judgement.

One December morning, Mistress Rebecca directed Henry and Nina to take up the painted floor cloth in the dining room. They were to drag it outside for America and Harriet to wipe and sponge off with mild soapy water. As it was drying, Nina and America scrubbed and waxed the varnished floor of the dining room. Then the floor of the front parlor was scrubbed after the woven wool rug was carried outside to be beaten, brushed, and aired in the sunshine.

Another day, Henry and Reuben were put to work brushing and scouring the firebox and hearth of the kitchen fireplace. America, Nina, and Harriet assisted that cleaning endeavor by sweeping up after them and then scrubbing and waxing the floor. Sarah, Willie, and David were stationed at the back door to fetch rags, brushes, or cleaning materials and hold the door open for worker movement in and out. The whole process proved to be very disagreeable: grease, burnt food, dirt, dust, and ashes had to be scrubbed off and disposed. By late morning, the scoured and scrubbed kitchen fireplace was returned to good working order. The workers, black and white, stopped their labor to get ready for the midday meal.

"Harriet, your skin matches America's." Sarah noticed that the grime on Harriet's hands and arms, and even the smudges on her face were close to America's skin color. "You could be a slave like America." Her solemn statement revealed her admiration for the light-skinned hired servant, as well as the fact that she had not been schooled in the idea of white superiority. The bustle of meal preparation slowed as everyone listened.

"No, Sarah. I do not wish to be a slave," Harriet informed her sister. "I would rather be a housewife, or a writer, or a teacher, or a seamstress." Harriet gave her answer as if she could choose an occupation for herself as a grownup. "And, I can wash this dark color off my skin. America can't. She was born dark just as we were born white."

Sarah understood that fact, but wished to carry it further. She turned to America. "If you could, would you wash the color off your skin?"

"No, Sarah." America inspected her soapy fingers and arms. "I am used to my skin." She smiled at the young girl and took a deep breath. She could feel the silent interest in the conversation, hovering in the kitchen like the steam of washday laundry. "I wish I could wash off the idea that slaves who are dark-skinned people, are lazy and dumb like animals." America dried her hands. "And, like your sister, I would rather be a housewife or a teacher."

"Me too." Sarah had closed the subject.

⚜ ⚜ ⚜

Jeremiah, coming for his last business visit of the year, agreed to extend America's contract to include the Christmas holiday. Master Murphy found America in the kitchen polishing the Tanner silverware and motioned for her to come outside with him.

"Merry, I have agreed that you will be here for Master Branch's Christmas feast." He paused, and then went on to tell her that he would come a few days after Christmas to bring her home before the New Year day. "You can celebrate the turn of the year in Lexington before going back to work at the Tanners. I have renegotiated the contract for next year."

America had anticipated her time off between Christmas and New Year as befitted most of the hired slaves. Even though she had not worked the regular contract time from January 1 to December 25, she thought Papa would make arrangements for her to return home for the Christmas break.

"Oh, Papa," America showed her disappointment. "I was looking forward to the Christmas doings in the neighborhood, going to the dance and patting juba. For once I would have an escort besides Mama, as I expect Jerry to be at his Master Abraham Skillman's house that week."

"Well, it cannot be helped." Jeremiah gave a shrug, apparently showing a lack of care for America's preferences. "Do not bite the hand that feeds you." America realized then that she was part of his business obligations.

As usual, America tried to find a positive outcome. *Maybe Papa is trying to get me used to life as an enslaved woman instead a favored daughter.* "More than likely I will still see Jerry when I do get to Lexington. Do you know if there are plans for a New Year celebration?"

"I do not know, but will ask Anne, as she talks to the neighbors more than I."

"I will talk to Jerry next Sunday. He might know some news about the doings in Lexington." America studied her papa, wondering if he was interested in Jerry's visits. She decided to let Jeremiah know, just to advance his understanding of her interest in him. "Jerry is helping me with reading and he has made friends with Henry and his son, Willie. On Sundays, we sit in the barn, and he reads the Bible aloud, as I follow the words. I use the nursery-rhyme book you brought, and Jerry hopes to borrow a schoolbook from Mister Crocket at Master John Skillman's place." She could not read his thoughts but continued. "Willie and I are learning more every Sunday. Henry helps anyway he can, although he is not interested in learning to read. He is more protective now, not as much of a tease as he once was."

"I am glad to hear that. It seems you have settled here nicely." Jeremiah grinned proudly, knowing that it was his decision to lease America out to Branch Tanner. Then, he paused to collect his thoughts. "Your mama was worried when I told her that Henry was one of the slaves you had met. 'She could come to harm!' Anne said. But, she knows Jerry and Aunt Dicy are on your side and will look out for you. She will be happy to know that your life follows her idea of making the best of what you have, besides being grateful for the circumstances." He had to hint that he was responsible for America's good fortune.

"Yes, Papa." America looked around for casual onlookers. When seeing none, she stretched up to give him a kiss on the cheek, displaying her happiness despite the news that she would miss the Christmas dance in Lexington. "Will you come on the Wednesday to bring me home after Christmas?"

"Probably. I do not know exactly. Just be ready to go when you see me. It might be Thursday." Jeremiah hoisted himself up to the driver's seat of the small carriage and shook the reins to let the horse know that forward movement was intended.

"Happy Christmas, Master Murphy! Fare thee well!" America returned to her work. She had accomplished quite a bit since November but had much to do before the Tanner Christmas feast.

The following Sunday, America told Jerry about Jeremiah's arrangement with Master Tanner for her to be at Pleasant Green Hill farm on Christmas day. "Papa will bring me back home after Christmas. I will not be in Lexington to enjoy the food and the dancing and the merriment of the day."

"Ah, merriment." Jerry chuckled. "Just listen to your name. You, Merry, are meant for merrymaking!" He laughed out loud, not just at the play with her name, but for information he was about to tell her. "There will be a wedding on the Saturday between Christmas and the New Year. Daniel who is owned by John Hunt Morgan for his rope walk, is marrying Hannah, the maidservant of Widow Lucretia Clay. She was manumitted in Henry Clay's will two years ago."

"Which means that any children they have will be born free." America smiled at that prospect.

"You would be correct in that assumption. And, may I assume that you would accompany me to the wedding dance and feast on Saturday, December 30?" Jerry raised his eyebrows with the suggestion, knowing full well what America's answer would be.

"With pleasure, Mister Jerry Burns. Thank you." America dipped a slight curtsy. "Where will the wedding take place?"

"Henry Clay's Ashland farm on the edge of town, which now belongs to James Clay. When I served Master Abraham in Lexington, I learned that Master James planned to renovate the old estate. The grounds of the home will be a good place for a wedding celebration as the family has moved out of the house, in preparation for the repairs and revisions."

Contemplating the circumstances, America had second thoughts. "Do you know Daniel or Hannah?" Having learned not to cross etiquette boundaries, she would not attend such an event unless she was a welcomed guest.

"Yes. I am looking forward to seeing the place and visiting with Daniel. I made his acquaintance as we helped fight the warehouse fire last summer. He gave me some ideas for repairs to Master Abraham's wagon. I expect Cook and Aunt Bette from Hopemont to be there, too, to help with the food, since Daniel is a favored servant. He is responsible for the upkeep of the spinning machines and looms necessary in the Morgan rope factory."

"Oh, Jerry. We should have a wonderful time! I can hardly wait for that day."

America had plenty to do until then. Mistress Rebecca saw to it that every part of the house sparkled in time for the guests who would arrive Christmas day. As she scrubbed woodwork and windows, America imagined that servants at Hopemont were similarly occupied. When she soaked and starched the lace curtains and attached them to curtain stretchers, she knew her mama, as a hired laundress, would sometime be employed at the same task, although curtain washing usually occurred in the spring. The Tanner curtains were in an especially sorry state. The summer's heat necessitated open windows that allowed blowing dust and dirt to invade the lace curtains of the front parlor and dining room.

Using leftover bits of printed calico and osnaburg, America had sewn many small pouches as she sat in the evenings near the fireplace in the slave cabin. She and Aunt Dicy filled them with dried herbs: mostly lavender, with pinches of rosemary and sage, securing them with braided wool. The fragrant little bags would be sachets for Mistress Rebecca on Christmas day. Rose had made lemon-flavored honey drops dusted with arrowroot powder. When the flattened disks were dry and hard, she and Nina put the sweet lozenges in folded fabric envelope bags that America had also sewn from pieces of brown Lowell cloth. The packets were to be given to Master Branch on Christmas morning. She saved back some of the honey drops to give to Jerry, knowing that his throat was still sensitive from the effects of the warehouse fire.

"Girl, we usually give Master and Mistress something at Christmas time. They are kind people, and they usually gift us with some treat." Aunt Dicy finished placing the sachets in a basket, ready to take over to the house on Christmas morning. "Oftentimes, we bring them something from the woods or henhouse, though. These little fabric pouches will surprise and should please them."

"They should be surprised." America was still somewhat disappointed that her Christmas break would be shortened. "I have never been at a big house on Christmas and was hoping that I would be home with Mama and Papa this time, too. But, as Papa said, it cannot be helped." She sighed and then looked at Aunt Dicy. "Mistress Rebecca should be pleased with all the work we have done since November. The house looks pretty, tidy, and clean!"

"Yes, child. You have made a difference in this house with your hard work and calm attitude. It has not been lost on Mistress Rebecca."

"What sort of treat do you think we will get?" America decided that now was the moment to ask.

"I do not know. Mistress almost always hands over new fabric and wool yarn to us women slaves so we can make our own clothes." Aunt Dicy frowned. "Huh. She acts like the material is a gift. It means more sewing and handwork for me, as well as for Rose and Nina." Aunt Dicy was not pleased with that anticipated circumstance. "That fabric is not a gift as far as I am concerned. It is a necessity."

"I can see that. My lease contract states that my clothes will be provided by Master Murphy. He wrote that in so Mama and I could choose the material and make clothes that fit. Now, I am glad he did that, although he has to pay for the fabric that Mama and I use." She chuckled at the fact that he would be paying for her well-being instead of just taking all the profit of her labor. "Papa is a kind master and sometimes he surprises me."

"Mistress Rebecca is a kind owner, and she has surprised us with special gifts at Christmas." Aunt Dicy nodded. "We will just have to wait until Christmas morning."

And, it wasn't a long wait. Since the house was now in order, the women and girls directed their attention to the upcoming dinner for the extended Tanner family. The best table linens were washed, ironed, and correctly folded to be set out at the right moment. America had already polished all the silverware, but the family's heirloom china service had to be counted and inspected to accommodate the generous dinner feast. Of course, tables and chairs had to be repositioned and arranged so that the Tanner adults as well as children could comfortably partake the meal.

Finally, Christmas day arrived. "Christmas gift! Christmas gift!" It was Willie's voice at the side door of the Tanner home that heralded the beginning of the special day. Master Branch and Reuben opened the door, inviting the male slaves into the dining room. The mantle was garlanded with pine branches lashed with strips of red bunting. The sideboard held a large punchbowl full of frothy eggnog. Master ladled the sweet nutmeg-spiced drink one cup at a time, poured a measured amount of bourbon into it, if the recipient was adult, and handed the drink to each male who stood at attention, waiting.

"I propose a toast to all my fine workers." Master Branch held his own cup. "In spite of the drought, you got the crops in, saw after the livestock, and kept the land in good order. Here's to you." He raised the cup and then took his first gulp. It was the signal for the servants, as well as Reuben and David, to take a drink from the cup they held. After a few more statements of encouragement and cup refills, Master Branch cleared his throat to address the small crowd of males. "As custom will have it, Willie gets the first Christmas gift because we heard him first. We thought he would be the first, so we prepared a surprise for him. Reuben and David, bring the gift."

Reuben put his cup down and reached under the table to pull out a stack of four, six-inch round rope coils. David held up two wooden spikes. "Here, Willie, we can play quoits." They held the set out to the young boy.

Willie shyly came over to Reuben. "Is this mine to keep?" Willie didn't know how to act when receiving a gift, and Reuben and David hadn't been trained in the art of graciously giving a gift. Silence interrupted the companionable gathering.

"The quoits are yours, Willie, to play with Reuben and David. Henry made the rings from those old rope pieces." Master Branch motioned to the gift with his eggnog cup. "Now, I think we have enough 'nog for another round. Then, I will hand out a gift to each of you."

The new shirts and pants for the men were stacked in a wide laundry basket tucked next to the sideboard. The hired slaves lined up to receive their sets of clothing and were invited to take an apple and a loaf of iced gingerbread arranged on the sideboard next to the large eggnog bowl.

The women and girls gathered in the front parlor. As expected, Mistress Rebecca gave Rose, Nina, and Dicy their fabric allotment. Each woman received a large folded rectangle of fabric pieces, tied with ribbon. Harriet brought out a much smaller, flattened fabric rectangle, tied up in ribbon similar to the other bundles.

At Mistress's nod, her daughter handed it to America. "I'm sure my folks knew what they would be getting, but this is a surprise for you, America." Mistress Rebecca motioned to the gift. "The fabric covers a piece of a book. Harriet found it at church, half of the book of hymns we use each Sunday. We do not know why it was separated from the first part, but what you have is Part Two of the book. Reverend Francis gave permission for us to have it. It has the words of church songs. The pages are still sewn together, but Harriet fashioned a cover for it."

"Oh, Mistress Rebecca and Harriet!" America hugged the book to her chest. "This is surely a Christmas surprise. Thank you!" Overjoyed to be in possession of another book, America did not know what else to say. She opened the book to see if she recognized any words or songs. Not finding any familiar songs, she knew Jerry would help her understand the printed words.

"We have a surprise for Rose, Nina, and Dicy." Mistress nodded to Sarah this time. "Sarah, bring out the basket you have been hiding."

Her youngest daughter pulled a lidded basket into view. When Nina lifted the lid, she saw two pairs of leather clogs and a pair of upholstery fabric slippers. "These shoes should be better than those wooden slippers. You will have to break them in for a while so they will fit each foot, but they should be just the thing for cold weather. Aunt Dicy, the fabric slippers should keep your toes toasty."

"Thank you, Mistress Rebecca, for thinking of my toes!" Aunt Dicy added a bit of humor to her gratitude for any creature comforts the Tanners could give.

"Thank you for the leather shoes." Rose pictured herself going out in the cold weather protected by the flexible footwear her new shoes provided.

"Thank you, Mistress Rebecca." Nina would be going to church in her new shoes, giving her feet a proper profile.

"We have a surprise for you and for Master Branch," Rose made this announcement. Nina hurried to get the basket from the kitchen, and then rushed back to hand over the basket to Mistress Rebecca. "Happy Christmas, Mistress Rebecca." Rose spoke for the enslaved women.

"Oh, sachets! They smell so clean and pure. Here, Harriet, just sniff this one. It is like it came straight from Aunt Dicy's garden."

"It did." America and Aunt Dicy sang the two word reply in harmony, then laughed at the accidental sound.

"And you made enough for almost every drawer we have for underclothes and sleepwear." Mistress Rebecca was obviously pleased. "Sarah can decide which sachet goes where. And what are these flat rectangles of fabric?"

"Those are for Master Branch." Rose smiled at her personally manufactured lozenges. "They hold lemon honey drops to soothe his throat."

"How nice. I am sure he will approve of those!" Mistress Rebecca looked around. "Now that our Christmas gift giving is over, we need to ready this parlor and dining room for our guests. Thank you for all the extra work."

"Thank you, Mistress." Rose, Nina, Aunt Dicy, and America again spoke in unison.

The Christmas dinner was accomplished without any unforeseen troubles. Servants attended to their masters, animals were taken care of, and slave and white children played together as they customarily did. Willie and Reuben shared their knowledge of quoits with the visiting Tanner youngsters. The day passed quickly, and the evening came soon with the shortened daylight hours. Because of all the extra responsibilities, America was almost too exhausted to enjoy what came next.

After the Branch Tanner servants saw to the needs of the family and their guests, they withdrew to the barn where Henry had cleared a large area inside for the good times. He and Willie had dragged short logs and stumps near the large opened barn door for seating outside, close by. Ample supplies of food left over from the midday feast were enhanced by special favorites brought by visiting slaves. Sweet potato fritters, possum meat pies, squirrel stew, and hoe cakes were spread out on the flat bed of the farm wagon as a makeshift table, covered by a clean cloth.

A slave owned by David Tanner in the neighboring farm, brought his gourd fiddle to play. Someone brought a wooden pipe flute and another visitor brought a drumming stick to amplify the rhythm. The festivities began when the music started. Many of the enslaved women and girls hummed and swayed to the flute and fiddle music, slowly adding their voices to well-known songs. One couple grasped hands and paraded around the circle in a lively promenade, as an invitation to other like-minded visitors. Soon the barn was filled with conversation, laughter, music, and dance.

Aunt Dicy was settled in a place of honor near the door of the barn. She was able to view all the activity, and each person who came paid respect to her. A dried mugwort concoction was her contribution to the gathering. People felt free to talk, seek counsel, complain, and make plans in her presence, calmed by the effect of the smoldering herb she arranged near her chair.

Other members of the group reveled in their freedom to step, twirl, prance, giggle, and mimic, surrounded by their peers. They patted juba, listened to stories, and interrupted the eating and fun with periods of dancing. The merrymaking continued into the small hours of the day. Slaves who came with families living farther away had to leave sooner to attend to the demands of the people who owned them. Tanner slaves, who lived within walking distance, kept up the celebration almost until dawn. America had retired to her cabin with Aunt Dicy after helping herself to modest portions of the feast in the barn. They each went to sleep, lulled into semi-consciousness by the music of the fiddle and flute, remembering the stories that were told, punctuated by the drumming stick. Rose and Nina stayed at the barn until the last visitor said goodbye.

Chapter 24
Good times

TWO DAYS LATER, JEREMIAH CAME TO SETTLE accounts with Master Branch and to bring America back home to Lexington. Her toil provided a thirty-dollar payment for him. Anne gave her daughter a warm welcome hug and then set about cooking a meal. She included all of America's favorite foods: greens flavored with ham hocks, mashed-potato pancakes, creamy grits, and a dessert of crumbled sweet cornbread, light sorghum, and buttermilk. America was glad to be home and to visit with her mama.

After they had cleared the table and put the kitchen in order and Jeremiah had retired to the middle room, Anne asked America about working as a full-time house servant. "Did anyone try to harm you? Impose his will on you?"

"No, Mama," America's voice reassured her. "There is one worker, Henry, who looks after the animals and the barn and runs errands for Master Branch. He teased me, but I stood up to him and was brave enough to outsmart him with words. When Jerry came, he soon figured out that Henry could be a threat, so he let him know that misbehaving with me would not be tolerated." She paused to appreciate that Jerry was a long-distance guardian. "I have come to think that Henry is lonesome. His wife was sold away, but he has an eight-year-old son. He seems to want adult connections."

"Being lonesome is no excuse for imposing one's will," Anne interrupted America's talk. She was adamant in her opinion.

"Mama, he and Jerry have come to an understanding and they have reached an agreement that is beneficial to everybody. Henry will watch out for anyone who might harm me, and, in return, Jerry will help Henry's son, Willie, learn to read while he helps me."

"That has put my mind to rest. And Master Branch? Is he a danger? How do the other servants treat you?" Mama was still worried about America's circumstances.

"I do not see much of Master Branch. He is busy tending to his family's holdings. Mistress Rebecca is nice. I help the girls with sewing, and Harriet, the oldest, helps me with reading, although we do not have much time to play school. I help Rose and Nina in the kitchen and do a lot of mending and laundry and cleaning, when time permits. There is a lot of work to do."

"Well, the more you can do for the masters and mistresses, the happier they are to have you."

"Mama, there is another servant: Aunt Dicy. She is like a grandmother. She keeps a garden behind the cabin and grows herbs. The thyme I sent you was from her garden. She helps in the kitchen and sees after the girls. She seems to know what will happen next." America stopped and took a good look at Anne. *Mama looks tired. Is she overworked now that I am not here to help her? Is she sad that I have found my way in the world and do not require her support?*

"Well, Mama, you can see that Papa found a good place for me. I am content there, but I do miss you. All the sayings and bits of wisdom, besides your way with a needle. The Tanners like what I have sewn, but I cannot hold a candle-or a needle!-to your abilities."

"Oh, Merry! I do miss you." Anne's soft voice almost squeaked as she talked. "I know you have to be out, serving other masters. But things are not the same with you gone."

"I am here right now. We need to make the most of our time together." America seemed to take the lead in getting over the sadness. "Would you help me fashion something to wear to the wedding celebration tomorrow evening? I will be going with Jerry."

"Yes. It will be fun to share some sewing chores with you." Suddenly, Anne remembered. Her expression changed: worry lines disappeared in her smile. "I have a dress set that a mistress handed down to me. She had outgrown the style and the color never did suit her looks, so I was glad to get it. The fabric is beautiful. We will need to get right to work on it, if it is to be ready by Saturday evening. How do you know Daniel and Hannah?"

"Well, Mama, Jerry knows Daniel. I did not want to go unless we were welcomed guests. How did you learn about the party?" America was pleased that her mama would help design a dress set she could use for the upcoming party-and for future occasions.

"Word gets around fast if it is either sadness or gladness. Uncle Eli heard it from Cook. The Hunt Morgans will be laying out the food for the feast. Daniel, even though he is a slave right now, is high up as a skilled workman in charge of all the machinery for the factory. He oversees many of the hired help. John Hunt Morgan likes Daniel and wants to keep him on. So, he told Aunt Bette to arrange for the viands at Ashland farm, which, of course, meant Cook would provide the food fixings."

"Hannah must be flattered that the Hunt Morgans are taking an interest in her wedding." America could not help but dip into the gossip of the day.

"Hannah is on the uppity side. I guess you would have to be to tend to Mistress Lucretia Clay. Hannah serves her night and day. She is free colored, but she works like a slave. She and Daniel will be living in a cabin on the James Clay property to serve Mistress Lucretia until Ashland house is finished and Mistress can move back." Anne was satisfied to give America the details.

"Since no whites live on that Clay estate right now, Mistress Lucretia must have given permission for Daniel and Hannah to have their doings on the grounds."

"She must have." Anne wanted to see if the cast-off dress would suit America. She had been saving the set to surprise her daughter, and now the wedding celebration would be the best opportunity to use it. And, they would be working on it together.

She went to the small wardrobe in the middle room. "Master Murphy," she addressed him formally with a smile. "We are here to retrieve a valuable, and will not disturb your reading. If you are curious, you are welcome to come to our design chamber in the next room to see and give judgment on our treasure." Anne gave him a bow as America chuckled.

"With pleasure, madam," Jeremiah responded in kind and then left the women to their sewing enterprise.

America held the fabric of the skirt up to her face. It was a lightweight brocade, dyed to a lustrous turquoise color. "Mama, I like the soft feel of this material. I think it will hang in pretty folds on my figure. Is the color right?"

"Yes, child. That color is becoming. Your dark hair and eyes shine back in the light of that rich blue-green. I always thought reds and yellows were the best with your tawny looks, but this brings out your beauty."

"Since it is in two pieces, I can work on one piece and you on the other. I will make a deep hem in the skirt and take in the waist. Will you fit the bodice to me and adjust it to size?" America took charge of planning the sewing task. "What can we do to give the dress set some interest?

Ribbons and lace are too expensive. Would Moses Spencer have any leftover trim in his secondhand store?"

"I doubt it. He only trades in used household items. If he had any lace curtains, it would take a lot of work to turn them into decorative trim. I could crochet or tat some lace, but we do not have the time." Anne shook her head, and then stopped abruptly in thought. "We could make our own." She was firm in that statement. Then, waxing philosophical, she winked at her daughter. "Necessity is the mother of invention."

Wanting to prove her worth as a designer, Anne continued, "Instead of hemming the skirt, you could make some rows of fabric tucks to go around the bottom of the dress, giving it a finished look. I could sew a white insert in the bosom of the bodice and at the cuffs of the sleeves. We could embroider flowers, vines, and leaves on the white pieces, and if there is time, do the same embroidery down the front of the dress's skirt!"

"That sounds wonderful, Mama. If I remember correctly, we had quite a variety of colored floss we used to mark pieces for the laundry. We can start right now. Maybe I should sew the tucking rows on the skirt while you put the white insert in the bodice and on the sleeve ends. You will have to fit it to me as you go. I can be a fine lady consulting a dressmaker. When we see that the whole set fits me from top to bottom, then we can decorate it with embroidery-like putting icing on a cake!"

America stopped to consider her good luck. "I am so pleased that I will have a new dress to wear. I think Jerry will like it too."

"You are taken with him, I can tell, Merry," Anne stated the obvious as her way of questioning America's intentions. "Of course, I should have known that by the way you always got ready for his visits here and the way you fashioned that message to him-with Papa's help." She smiled encouragement.

"Yes, Mama," America nodded. "I was interested in him from the time he brought that package of books to Master Calvin Morgan at Hopemont." America smiled but did not say any more.

Working steadily that evening and through the next two days, Anne and America finished refurbishing the dress by late afternoon Saturday. It fit well and the greenish blue was a favorable accent to America's color. "Even though this is not a ball gown, I feel like Cinderella, and you, Mama, are my fairy godmother." America whispered this as she pulled on her new dress in the privacy of the middle room of the small house.

When Jerry arrived, he was favorably impressed, as was Jeremiah who decided not to demand all the attention he was usually afforded as head of the house. The weather was mild considering the time of year, so America utilized the crimson, woolen shawl that Anne had fashioned for her last year.

"Enjoy yourselves and the friends you see." Jeremiah was quick to send them on their way.

"You know the food that Cook furnishes will be top of the line. And, you will have to heed the rhythm and pat juba!" Mama added encouragement to her sometimes shy daughter.

Jerry and America entered into the merrymaking as soon as their walk led them to Ashland farm on the outskirts of Lexington. They heard the fiddle and flute before they saw the wedding celebrants among the trees. A large group encircled the lively dancers, patting juba and yelling encouragement. "Hambone, Hambone, where ya' been?" they sang, accompanied by the slapping rhythm.

"Around the world and back again." Others answered in the same beat made by hitting their thighs and chest. Jerry and America both clapped their hands in rhythm as they walked toward the group of revelers. Jerry soon started patting juba as America clapped and kept time with her feet.

She spied Uncle Eli helping Cook transfer the baskets and crocks from the service wagon to the tables, although she was too far away to greet them. There were people gathering to meet and greet acquaintances, children chasing each other across the broad lawn, and older, more sedate friends waiting for the official ceremony to begin. The white attendees were treated with respect and deference.

The object of most of the older guests' attention was the beautifully decorated wedding cake. It shared a linen-covered table with three large pitchers of fruit-juice enhanced teas surrounded by cups, saucers, forks, and napkins all on loan from the Hunt Morgan pantry. Cook had made the fruitcake, which was topped with a white glaze, dried cherries, sliced rounds of oranges, and daisy shapes made of almond slices.

The guests were attired in their Sunday best, although the actual day was Saturday. Jerry knew and recognized many more people than America, as he had been able to easily move around Lexington when he was the servant of bookseller Abraham Skillman. Finally, America caught the attention of Aunt Bette who had arrived with Uncle Eli on his second trip between Hopemont and Ashland. They bestowed a welcoming embrace and then called to Cook and Uncle Eli, who gathered around America and Jerry. Daniel, the guest of honor, joined the group, shaking Jerry's hand.

"Now, here is a groom. And not a horse in sight." Jerry could make fun as he often served as groom to Master Skillman's horses.

America, nibbling on a small johnnycake offered by Aunt Bette, appreciated his humor and just smiled at him. *He is not yet a bridegroom.*

"I am the groom this evening because Hannah and I wanted to take this time between the holidays to jump the broom. There's a little more freedom to celebrate before the calendar rolls around to January. Hannah was not sure she wanted to take part in jumping over a broom, but I convinced her. "

"Christmas is the freedom time for all of us." America, remembering the good times at the Tanner farm just a week ago, decided to join the conversation.

"For me, the rope walks and bagging machines are idle because the hemp is not ready to process yet, so I have some time to spend," Daniel explained. "Mistress Lucretia thought this date and place would be suitable as Ashland's house renovation had disrupted the Clay family anyhow."

"Everything is just beautiful, and the food is up to Hunt Morgan standards, Daniel," America added. She looked around for Hannah.

"Remember how valiantly we fought the warehouse fire?" Daniel had turned to Jerry. "I have never been so hot in my life! And when you stepped in to spell that poor devil who had sunk to his knees, I thought you were on your way to the River Jordan for sure."

"I am a tough workhorse. All of us just wanted to put out the fire." Jerry remembered his singed hair and skin. "Ah, here is the bride." Jerry took an appreciative look at Hannah and then smiled at America who had watched him. "You are the best-looking filly in this group, Merry." He said that in a whisper. "Besides, you bring merriment wherever you go."

"Is that straight from the horse's mouth, Mister Jerry Burns?" America had a quiet answer to his comment.

After introductions were made, Hannah had some news to share. "Do you remember 'King' Solomon here in Lexington?"

After a pause, Daniel spoke up. "Was he the gravedigger during the cholera of '33? I heard that he dug graves for many victims."

"Yes, Daniel." Hannah nodded. "London Ferrill also dug graves at that time, too. He was the preacher at the church I went to. He died this fall." Hannah stopped to swallow her grief for the former church leader. "Well, I just heard that 'King' Solomon died earlier this month."

"Did you know him?" Jerry came right to the point. America knew London Ferrill and how he was a friend of Jeremiah. *But, why bring up Solomon, the grave digger?*

"I did not know Solomon, but I just heard something strange." Hannah looked around her. "He was white and he was owned by a black woman, an Aunt Charlotte. She bought him at auction right before the cholera hit, in 1833."

"A black woman owning a white slave! Amazing!"

America turned to Uncle Eli who lingered nearby. "Did you know of Solomon?"

"Only that he was a drunkard and a tramp. Charlotte bought him at a bargain price that would just clear up his debts and pay for his jail upkeep. The city put him up for auction as a nuisance. Charlotte wanted his labor for her pie business. She bought him to work, and she took care of him." Uncle Eli knew more than the rest of them. "What he did during the epidemic was outstanding for a white man. And everybody heard about him at the time. I think it was his drinking that saved him. All that alcohol was like a cleanser for his insides."

"The other oddity is that the city had a memorial service for him a few weeks ago, and his body is buried in the new cemetery with all the other prominent citizens of our city, including John Wesley Hunt and Henry Clay!" Hannah was scandalized that a tramp would be honored along with all the distinguished residents.

"I wonder where Aunt Charlotte is buried." America's comment raised the question.

"Who cares? She probably died in the epidemic. Who is to know the records from back then." Hannah almost sniffed at America's wonderment.

America hid her disappointment with Hannah's attitude. It was almost like Miss Catherine's dismissal of information that did not fit her opinions. *Except Hannah is black. Even though she is free, she should understand the double standard we face every day.*

On the walk back home on Upper Street, America contemplated the good times.

"A penny for your thoughts, Merry." Jerry noticed that she was exceptionally quiet.

"I was just thinking about how we always oblige the masters and make the best of the circumstances. We adjust and move on. Jerry, you and I both have no say in what is to become of us." Folding the shawl around her shoulders in frustration, she touched the bodice of her dress and then held out the skirt from her body. "Even this dress is a make-do since there is no money to buy new. Patting juba is our tradition of marking rhythm to songs and dances because, long ago, we were forbidden to have drums. Did you know that?"

"Well, Miss Merry, I have become Master Make-do. Any wish you wish will be a wistful want. I promise to see about it." Jerry's tongue sought his cheek.

As America rolled her eyes at his pronouncement, she caught a glimpse of the North Star. "Look! It is the same star I see on clear nights at the Tanner farm."

"That it is," Jerry replied, squinting through the evergreens to see it. "Want to leave a wish on it?"

"It is a reminder to me right now that I want to work on your quilt. Since I left the pieces in Aunt Dicy's care, I will just work on a star piece at this time. It will be in the center. What color do you think it should be?"

188

"I like the color of your dress. Do you have any leftover fabric to make a star shape?"

He said just the right thing.

"Yes, Master Make-do. I promise to see about it. Now, I must bid you adieu. Sleep well and I will see you tomorrow." America gave him a lingering kiss that kept him warm all the way to Master Skillman's quarters.

"Papa, I have come to a realization." America brewed some tea for him, as she prepared the breakfast grits and shaved ham for gravy.

"Yes, Merry, Merry, not contrary. What have you been thinking?"

"I heard last night that 'King' Solomon died. I am sure you knew of him."

Jeremiah nodded.

"He dug graves for victims of the cholera in 1833. When he died this month, the city had a memorial for him. They buried him in the new cemetery."

Jeremiah nodded.

"Did you know he was white and was owned by a black woman named Aunt Charlotte?"

Jeremiah nodded, again. "Yes, Merry. It is unusual. What are you getting at?" He thought she had exhausted her supply of information without coming to the point.

"Nobody knows anything about Charlotte other than she was free colored. She paid for him as a way to free him from his debts and to relieve the city of a nuisance. She must have given him shelter and food to sustain him to be able to dig graves for so many people who died. They call him a hero of the cholera epidemic. But he could not have done what he did without her care and support. Nobody knows when she died or where she is buried."

"You are probably right. But what do you want to tell me?" At that moment, Papa's name could have been Jeremiah Impatient Murphy.

"I have come to realize that color rules, as you mentioned months ago. We are judged by our skin color. Charlotte would never have been buried in the new cemetery with all the white folk. No one even knows where her resting place is. Solomon, an alcoholic vagrant, was buried with honor in the white cemetery."

"Now, Merry, they buried London Ferrill in that new cemetery. All the prominent families have plots there. He was a black man buried in a white cemetery. That refutes what you just said."

"Oh, Papa, London Ferrill probably had more white friends than you do. He worked at making friends and influencing whites and blacks. He was honored by the white leaders of Lexington." America stirred the grits in the pan, adding a little salt and butter to flavor it. The awareness of skin color bubbled and hissed in her mind like the cooking task she was managing.

"Rightfully so." Jeremiah was quick to defend his departed friend.

"What I wish to point out is that all three, London Ferrill, Aunt Charlotte, and 'King' Solomon, are remembered because they did something out of the ordinary. They proved their worth. To me, it is interesting that Charlotte and London were slaves who bought their freedom and worked hard to make something of themselves. Solomon was born free, but he gave his freedom away to alcohol." She sighed. "I am born a slave and have worked at bettering myself."

"I know that, Merry. I am glad you are my daughter." Jeremiah appeared to be relieved at what America was saying, even if he did not share her passion for the pathway to improvement.

"It is easy for me to know and do the proper things because you and Mama taught me right." America paused to realize that she clarified her thinking by talking. "There are many more slaves who do not know how to better themselves. Aunt Charlotte and London Ferrill did. But, most slaves do not have a black co-worker who will teach and guide them."

"That is for sure." Jeremiah agreed with America and was thankful that Anne had been so successful raising their daughter.

America continued her thought. "Aunt Charlotte has been forgotten for her kindness to 'King' Solomon. She will only be pointed out as that black woman who bought a white man at auction, making her a novelty in a world where color rules. 'King' Solomon, on the other hand, was honored as the gravedigger who showed his compassion for the white families of cholera victims that year. Color is too powerful. It can make or break an individual."

America remembered the twin foals from John Wesley Hunt's farm. They were likely selected to be coach horses because of their matching chestnut coats. *They were broken to harness to obey their driver's commands.*

She thought of Miss Catherine, a privileged member of the white Hunt Morgan family, who talked about her Frankfort house servant, Mattie, complaining that she was too subservient. *More than likely, Mattie had been trained that way in order to survive as a slave.*

And, America could not forget the terror of her own kidnapping. *I had been snatched because of my skin color with the real possibility of breaking my spirit. If the kidnapper had been successful, I could have been sold to spend the rest of my life as a fancy girl.*

"Somehow, the world will have to understand that a person's worth should be judged by their actions and fortitude, not by the color of their skin." America punctuated her statement with a wave of the long cooking spoon.

"Amen." Jeremiah smiled at her for the first time that morning. His pronouncement brought her back to the present. "Merry, Merry, not contrary, how does your garden grow?"

"With silver bells, and magic spells, and bright colors all in a row." America's smiling response seemed to be the perfect antidote to their underlying anxiety about what the coming years would bring and the necessary changes that would be required.

Chapter 25
A New Year

JEREMIAH AND AMERICA STARTED THE JOURNEY BACK to Pleasant Green Hill farm on Tuesday, the day after New Year. The renovated brougham held no fright for Merry any more, and she was pleased to be out in the crisp morning air.

Slaves, walking the streets to their relegated places of work in Lexington, rubbed sleep from their faces, masking a few stoic tears. Their walk was purposeful in the morning sunlight, as they prepared themselves to begin another year of bondage. The good times of the week before was only a respite from labor as chattel. Many slaveholders used that time to readjust their slave populations, selling some individuals and renting out others. Economy measures browbeat social standing and color distinction. Uncertainty was around every corner.

Wearing a newly made blue linsey-woolsey dress under her woolen shawl, Merry clutched the small carpetbag. Her satchel now contained the blue-green dress set she and Anne worked on during her short visit and the quilt square she had cut from leftover fabric. Anxious to show and tell Aunt Dicy about her activities, she was nevertheless unhappy to part with Anne. Breakfast that morning was painfully quiet. Both women understood that responsibilities had to be met, and Anne was already dressed to tend to her laundry work. But, what hung over their demeanor was the sadness that it would be a year before they would see each other again. Anne put on a brave face as she kissed America goodbye.

Jeremiah also possessed an article of importance. Folded inside the pocket of his dark wool suit coat was the agreed upon contract for America's hire for the coming year, ready for Branch Tanner's signature. If the year proved successful to the transaction, he would receive one hundred dollars in December. "Merry, Merry, not contrary. How did your week with Mama go?" He had modified the rhyme to fit his question. He was uncertain that the time between Christmas and New Year was beneficial to slave productivity; however, it was necessary to reset and renegotiate contracts.

"With a wedding broom, and wishes that bloom, and bright colors all in a row." Merry's smile was warm, but her answer was almost enigmatic. She had been contemplating her future with Jerry but knew Papa would not be asking about their budding romance. Instead, he must have considered the week at home to be a gift from him, as a slaveholder, to Anne and America.

"Wedding broom?" He turned his attention away from the horse to study America's face.

"Papa, you have heard of slaves who get married by jumping the broom with everyone watching. It has been on my mind since Hannah and Daniel's wedding."

"Ahhh." He smiled. "Slave weddings can happen that way."

"Marriage among slaves is forbidden." America was telling him something he already knew. "But, if they want to live as husband and wife, they will have a ceremony like jumping the broom to show everyone they are going to live together at least part of the time."

"Yes, my girl." Jeremiah became thoughtful. He adjusted the reins to his comfort and rested one hand on the brake lever.

"Papa," America continued the thread of conversation. "If Jerry and I ever had a child, would you own it?"

"Yes. That topic came up in a conversation with Master Branch Tanner," he paused, cautiously trying to couch his thinking in business terms. "A child of a slave is owned by the slaveholder."

"If you had a conversation about that, then the two of you must be agreeable to me marrying Jerry." She stopped and took a sidelong look. "If he ever asks me."

"I think Jerry would be a good match for you, Merry. Any children you might have would be a blessing, just as you are to Anne and me."

"He has not brought up the question, but if he does, it is good to know that you and Master Tanner would approve the arrangement." *There. I will keep my own counsel on that subject. But Papa has no objections to Jerry! Hurrah!*

"You know that Jerry would have to get permission from the Skillmans, both Master Abraham and Master John." Jeremiah knew about negotiations with business agreements: all parties must be of one mind.

"Well, Master Murphy, I want to tell you that Jerry has not broached the subject, although his actions have lead me to think of the pleasant possibilities."

"Because both of you are hired out, marriage arrangements can be tenuous. Master Branch and I are both satisfied with your presence on his farm and with Jerry's visits. The Skillmans might have other thoughts, though."

"I guess I will just have to be patient. It is comforting to know that you approve of Jerry." America looked out at the dry, brittle, brown fields as the brougham sheltered them from the cold wind.

"Always have. He has given us many reasons to believe he is a suitable life partner for you."

※ ※ ※

When Jerry visited America the next Sunday, she handed him the blue-green quilt square as he mounted the horse to return to Willow Valley Farm. A white star had been appliqued with fine embroidery thread used to decorate and enhance the shape. Aunt Dicy had inspected America's handiwork and given her approval.

"Mister Jerry Burns, this is to show to your mama and tell her that I am in the process of making a quilt with the pieces she gave you. This square will be in the center of the quilt."

"She will surely be pleasantly surprised." Jerry took the square and gently placed it in the fabric pouch he carried across his shoulders that contained the travel pass written by Master John Skillman. "Mama is not in good health, but the news that you are making a quilt with those fabric pieces I had kept all these years should cheer her."

"I am honored that you placed them in my hands. Please bring this square back after your mama has seen it. Aunt Dicy helped me design a beautiful pattern for the squares and we will be quilting the pieces into a warm and comforting blanket."

"Comforting." Jerry gave America a shy smile. "That is what you are. The possibility of sheltering under the quilt blanket with you is indeed comforting to me in my present circumstances."

"Now, Jerry," America teased, remembering her first encounter with Jerry, using the wrong term for a book's cover. "Here is the difference between a cover and a blanket. A cover shelters sheets-paper or fabric. A blanket is a layer of warmth and protection. Is that correct?"

"Yes, Miss Merry Murphy." Jerry saluted her. "You have pretty much uncovered that mystery!"

"Perhaps, in the future, we can learn more about books and their covers together and solve other mysteries." America reverted to formal language. "I look forward to that prospect." *I would love to be sheltered in the warmth and protection of your arms, too!*

Jerry answered her statement with smiling eyes. "I must be on my way." He leaned down from the saddle of his workhorse partner to plant a quick kiss on her lips.

"Fare thee well! I hope to see you next Sunday!" Jerry was acquainted with America's parting words now. He almost repeated them back to her.

The next week, Jerry returned the appliqued quilt square, reporting that his mama was pleased to hear of the plans for it. "Her eyesight is failing. She held that blue-green fabric up close and inspected it out of the corners of her eyes. She felt all the edges and the embroidery threads of the star-shaped design. How she held that piece of fabric told me that Mistress Lydia will not be putting her to work at sewing. It was work that she used to enjoy."

"I am sorry to hear that, Jerry. I would think there is much she still can do in that house, though."

"Her knowledge of kitchen work is put to good use." Jerry offered that fact. "And she can handle the fancy washing. The hard work of hefting wet laundry is beyond her capabilities, though, but she knows how it should be done. She can teach the young girls."

"More than likely, she is glad you are back at Willow Valley Farm," America countered his statement. *Huh. I wonder how many of the young girls are glad you are on the farm. I need to solve that mystery myself!*

"I hope to make things easy for her." Jerry considered his options as he patted the horse's neck and stroked its mane. "Charles can help me, though he does not have the run of the farm like I do. He is considered a valuable field hand, useful for hard labor, and as a foreman in the barnyard."

"Your work is more like Henry's." America looked around for him and for Willie. "You can move around to different areas of the farm and are trusted to put things right."

"Did someone mention my name?" Henry appeared at the barn door, taking the reins of the workhorse Jerry had ridden. The two men unsaddled the horse and led him to a clean stall supplied with hay and grains in the manger. "Willie is toting in firewood for Rose. He will be coming along."

"I will get the books ready. Jerry, the Bible you borrowed from Master Skillman is still here. Will he want it back any time soon?" America tried to get the reading lesson under way so she would have more time later to spend with Jerry.

"I think Master Skillman approves of my use of it. I still have not borrowed the schoolbook from Mister Crocket, though." Jerry looked around to see if Henry was listening. He lowered his voice just in case the fellow slave should overhear what he had to say. "In the short times I have spent with Mister Crocket, we tend to discuss the news and the latest laws about fugitive slaves."

"Oh, Jerry. Do be careful." America, for all her understanding of Jerry's lawfulness and trusted mobility, was happy to understand that Mister Crocket seemingly looked out for Jerry's interests.

Willie walked in, brushing sawdust and bark from his arms and smoothing his hands down his shirt. When America looked at him disapprovingly, he turned back to dip his hands in the water trough outside and scrub his face and hands. The action showed his willingness to take part in his education and do the right thing.

"Thank you, Willie, for seeing that the books are kept clean and free of dust and dirt." America was beginning to enjoy the process of playing school, especially with Jerry alongside.

At the end of the reading lesson, America and Jerry walked around the barn to view the Tanner horses in their paddock and to see the hemp field. Jerry was already acquainted with the big house and the slave quarters, but he wished to see how Master Tanner had organized his holdings. Because the farm was almost self-sustaining, there was more to be seen in future visits. What caught his interest was the two-story brick building near the hemp field. His attention attracted America's interest.

"What is that building?" America squinted in the waning afternoon sun. "It looks like it has two floors. Do they put hemp in it?"

"I do not know, Merry." Jerry shook his head. "Since it is close by the hemp field, there must be a connection. Master Skillman does not have a building near any of his hemp. Charles might know."

"It looks like a dry, sturdy enclosure." America thought of possibilities that would involve private visits with Jerry. *Could we use that building as our secret dwelling?* She longed for her time spent exclusively with him.

"I must be on my way." Those words were Jerry's indication that he would be leaving soon. They walked back to the barn, saddled up the workhorse, enjoyed a long hug and quick kiss, and then Jerry got on the horse. He adjusted the reins and tipped his hat to America.

"Fare thee well! I hope to see you next Sunday!" They spoke the oft-used words in unison.

Chapter 26
Another New Year

THE FIRST SUNDAY OF THE COMING YEAR was January 6. In many ways, America's life had not changed much in the last twelve months. She attended to the needs of the Branch Tanner household, helping Rose and Nina with food preparation and service. Aunt Dicy was a comforting cabinmate as well as a grandmother figure. Mistress Rebecca and her children brought light and life to the family activities. America now had a positive attitude about Henry and his son Willie, thanks to the understanding that Jerry had established with him. Jerry had become an indispensable part of her life, coming over each Sunday afternoon to visit with her. Jeremiah showed up about once a month to check on her well-being and to do business with Master Tanner concerning his livery enterprise.

Her Christmas holiday break was spent back in Lexington, visiting Anne and seeing Jerry each day. He, too, had returned to Master Abraham Skillman's home in town on his holiday time off.

Jerry arrived late each Sunday visit to Pleasant Green Hill farm in that January. The weather had made travel by horseback treacherous, so Jerry set out on foot, wearing tough, durable, well-made boots. He followed the frozen surface of the creeks and streams each week, which made his travels easier but afforded little respite from the cold.

On the first Sunday in February, he was again atop his workhorse partner. Although happy to see America, he displayed a subdued, thoughtful demeanor. There was no gladsome hug or furtive kiss. He sat across the makeshift reading table in the stable. Usually his place was beside America.

Willie remarked on the change in Jerry's behavior. "Mister Jerry, are you going to read a Bible story instead of helping us try to make out the words? You look as frozen as the ice in the water trough."

"It is still cold out, but the horse has kept me warm as we made our way over." Jerry cleared his throat. "I will read a passage while you listen. Then I will hand over the Bible so the two of you can figure out the words together."

"All right, Mister Jerry Burns." America agreed to the seating arrangement but wondered what Jerry wanted to do after the lesson.

She soon found out.

"America, I want more than anything to have a child with you." He almost whispered the words as Willie left.

She stopped and smiled and put her hands on his arm as they exited the barn. "Oh, Jerry. I want…"

Jerry softly interrupted. "But I do not want a child born in slavery. I cannot allow any baby coming into this world as a slave."

"Jerry, my children would be…," America swallowed, crossed her arms, and stood very still, trying to control her thoughts and words. They walked along the pasture fence, keeping their voices low. "What are you trying to say?"

"A man and his wife escaped across the river to Ohio last month. They had their four children with them." He paused, allowing America to understand the information. She was confused. He continued. "Slave catchers tracked them down for the slave owner in Kentucky. As they locked up the family, the woman started to kill her children. She would rather see them die than be condemned to life as a slave. Her name is Margaret. She succeeded in killing one daughter but was stopped before she could do any more harm." Jerry shuddered as he told the story.

America gasped. Then, by voicing her confusion, she tried to make sense of Jerry's story. "What a horrible circumstance!" Then she remembered that someone might be listening. "And you do not want it to happen to us."

"Yes. I do not want to bring a child into this world of slavery." Jerry would not be convinced otherwise.

"But we are better off than most slaves. We could. . . " America did not continue her statement. She had seen Jerry's determined scowl before.

"If I could convince your father that your freedom is essential to our life together and I would see that you come to no harm, we could have children who would be free. Or, if I could purchase your freedom, our children would be free." Jerry quietly voiced what had been on his mind throughout his day's journey. Color rules freedom.

"But, Jerry, just because I might get free papers for me and our children," America stopped again. *We are talking about our children! Jerry is considering having children with me! How exciting!* She looked around. "does not mean that we will be treated differently. Our babies' skin color will indicate how they will be viewed. Too many people think white is free, black is slave!"

"Now, you have given me thoughts to contemplate on my way back to Willow Valley." Jerry lowered his voice again. "The story was in the Cincinnati paper that Mr. Crocket had. I put myself in that situation as I read and reread what happened. Robert Garner, Margaret's husband, must have witnessed all that went on. If I was there, I would not have let those slave catchers take my family. Margaret knew what would become of her children in the hands of her master. I would die trying to save my family."

"Those are strong words. I have no doubt you would carry out your intentions." America looked down at the fence rails. "But, we have been blessed with good owners, and we owe them honest labor for what they have provided."

"We do not owe them anything! These farms," he silently gestured at the pasture area, "are built with the blood and sweat of black slaves. Now, our state is known as a prime breeding area for slavery. Many masters want their female slaves to have children because they benefit from the ownership. Your papa is an exception. As a businessman, he has learned that honesty and truth are essential. He loves you and cherishes your mama."

"He still owns Mama and me."

"Yes. And I can understand why he still does, but that is another matter." Jerry knew that the conversation needed to end. He had made his point about raising a child in slavery. As a suitor, he wanted to enjoy America's company.

As the object of his affection, America was quite willing to change the subject of their discussion. They had reached the hemp field again. It was the turning point of most of the walks they had together over the last few months. At this time, the hemp house showed signs of activity: an open door and shutter, a dirt track as if something heavy had been dragged to and from the field, hemp stalks making a small stack near the doorway.

"Aahh, Merry." Jerry was his congenial self again. "I figured out why this building is here. It is for hemp cultivation."

"Yes, Mister Burns. I could have figured that out." America teased him by putting her arm through his. The cold wind blew her shawl over his shoulder.

Replacing the shawl onto her shoulder, he pointed to the only door in the building. "On that first floor, they would store equipment to harvest the hemp stalks and the brakes used to pound the stalks once they have softened some in the fields. Right now, the hemp brakes are put to use in the fields as we are doing for Master Skillman. Also, they probably keep the hemp seeds in a crib ready to be sown in the spring." Jerry pointed to the window of the floor above. "That loft is where they would put the broken hemp fibers until they are taken to market. Any extra space on the first floor would be used for leftover hemp bundles, too. That brick building is a sturdy, dry place to store the accumulated hemp as a cash crop for Master Tanner."

"You figured it out. Working in Master Skillman's hemp fields, you saw how the process is handled." America smiled in admiration.

"There is another reason for finding how the building is used." Jerry paused and glanced shyly at America. "Perhaps we could clean up a corner of it to use as our private shelter, maybe on the side opposite the hemp brakes. Do you think that is possible?"

"I think so. But, I will investigate possibilities. I will ask Aunt Dicy. Maybe you could check with Henry. Then we can talk with Master Tanner to get his permission." America concealed her enthusiasm by busying herself with her shawl and pushing her windblown hair off her forehead. *Jerry is talking about spending time with me in private! Oh, happy day!*

"I must be on my way." He turned to the barn for his workhorse partner. Henry had already saddled the horse for the trip home. Jerry chose not to ask Henry for information about the hemp house. That could wait for another day. He adjusted the reins and tipped his hat to America.

"Fare thee well! I hope to see you next Sunday!" They spoke the oft-used words in unison.

Chapter 27
Still another New Year

"AMERICA MURPHY, WILL YOU MARRY ME?" Jerry asked the question as soon as he dismounted from the workhorse in the barnyard of Pleasant Green Hill farm the following January. He stood with the reins in his hands waiting for her reply, although he was sure what it would be.

"What?" America took a step toward him, not sure she had heard right. Confusion collided with surprise on her face.

"Marry me." Jerry wished to erase her confusion.

"Yes!" America's answer was without any doubt. "When? Where? How?"

"Now, Merry. One step at a time." The workhorse dipped his head and took a step forward, as if to carry out Jerry's words.

"Yes, Jerry!" She leaned closer for a kiss. Still holding the reins, he grabbed her waist and lifted. Their embrace was swift, light, and joyful.

"I do not want another year go by without a course of action." Jerry looked around the area. "We have known each other for almost three years. Our pairing has been on my mind as far back as our encounter at the Morgan house."

"Yes, Jerry." America seemed to be at a loss for words other than 'yes.'

"I love you and I think you are likewise inclined."

"Yes, Jerry. I love you." America looked at her blue linsey dress and scuffed slave shoes. She tucked a strand of hair behind her ear. *I feel like a princess but surely do not look like one.* She glanced around the yard. Henry leaned against the door of the barn but did not advance to greet Jerry. There was Aunt Dicy at the kitchen window. Harriet, walking slowly to the chicken coop, egg basket in hand, silently regarded them with a bright smile. *They all know.*

"We need to make a plan." Jerry turned to see after the horse, leading him over to the barn to unsaddle, feed, and water: actions that came as second nature to him. Henry disappeared into the barn to straighten and tidy the designated area for reading lessons.

America waved at Aunt Dicy and then walked over to the chicken coop to assist Harriet. She glowed in anticipation of future events.

"Jerry must have had some wonderful news. I can see happiness on your face." Harriet wanted to share America's gladness.

"Yes. Maybe his visits will be longer. We are going to make plans for that. Does Rose need more eggs?" America quickly returned to everyday topics, as house servant duties dictated.

Harriet nodded and glanced at the few eggs she had collected. "I hope he can be here longer." She had already learned the art of gentle comradery from her mother, but the curiosity of youth had not escaped her. The trip to gather more eggs was a fact-finding endeavor. But America was happy to reveal her light-heartedness without jeopardizing Jerry's trust.

After the reading lesson with Willie, America and Jerry strolled past the ice-covered plank fence to the hemp house. The hemp brakes had been inspected and repaired, ready to be dragged out to the fields when the weather became more temperate. With Master Branch's permission, Jerry and America had fashioned a makeshift seating area in one corner facing the door, utilizing a large straw bundle and short rough-cut boards. The brick wall nearby was lined with stalks of hemp, which offered some warmth. It had become their haven of privacy.

As soon as they entered the building, Jerry gathered America in his arms for a long lingering kiss. "I hope there will be more of that in the years to come." America smiled at him with a shy satisfied look.

"You can count on that, my Merry." He walked around the area he and America had cleared and furnished. After two years of laboring in the hemp fields and seeing after the livestock, Jerry's physical abilities had strengthened. Farm life seemingly was beneficial to his health: he had developed good muscle tone and stamina. The cough that had plagued him since the warehouse fire was now gone.

"What will we do now to move things along for a wedding, Jerry?" America was practical. She knew marrying Jerry would involve four slave masters. "Papa has told me that you would be an acceptable husband, and I think Master Branch would not put up any protest to our arrangement."

"As far as I can tell, we could plan for me to come over on Saturdays, spend the night, and return to Willow Valley farm on Sunday evening, until I figure a way out of slavery for both of us," Jerry thought out loud.

"Spend the night here in the hemp house?"

"Yes, Merry."

America gave a happy sigh.

Jerry gazed through the door. "I need to get permission from Master Abraham and Master John. I would be away from Willow Valley on Saturdays and Sundays."

"And you think they would not like that you would be here all that time each weekend." America was trying to see the Skillman side of the arrangement.

"After all," Jerry replied, "Master John would not benefit. You know how the white folks want to control us. If we are not at their beck and call, they want to know why. Master John would not see any good in my absence those two days every week."

"How are we going to change his mind?"

"Merry, we will have to think long and hard about this." Jerry held her hands in both of his. He had some ideas but was committed to hearing more from America. "Would Master Branch have need of an extra hand? If Master Abraham hired me out to him, then I would be here all the time." They both smiled at that possibility, and together glanced around the hemp house, imagining it as their own permanent shelter. "That probably would not work. Henry does what I do at Willow Valley. There could not be two of us here at Pleasant Green Hill. I could be a field slave here, but they are usually hired out as a gang from one owner. The only slave that Master Abraham hires out is me."

"Do you think Papa would hire me out to Master John?" America considered the possibility and squinted at Jerry. *Mister Crocket boarded there as a schoolteacher, so there must be children in the household even though Jerry had never spoken of any.* "We would be together that way."

"Well," Jerry contemplated her idea. "I guess your papa is satisfied with the business he conducts with Master Branch besides hiring you out. There is the hay and grain he buys for his livery, and more than likely he has looked over horses that Master Branch breeds. I expect some time he will purchase some healthy stock to train as carriage horses. Your hire is a part of the good business relationship he has with Master Branch."

"Yes. And those are good reasons why I should stay here." Relief smoothed the worry wrinkles on America's face. "Aahhh, I have been so thought-filled about my own happiness, I am just now considering another situation. Is there a female servant in Master John's house that would be interested in Henry?"

"There are two likely women." Jerry did not elaborate.

"If Henry got along with one of them, perhaps Master John would appreciate the advantage of having him visit, as you do here. I know that Henry has been lonely these years since his wife was sold down the river."

"Some masters think of us as breeding stock, and Master John is probably in that group. If he can encourage his female slaves to have children, then he would increase his chattel. I will think on that perspective."

"My guess is that Master John has already considered that possibility as far as you are concerned. Surely, I am not the only one to admire your physic. You have filled out in your shoulders and chest." America boldly touched his arms and back.

"Am I a colt turning into a stallion?" Jerry teased. "All the sweat and strain in the hemp fields and pitching hay and pulling up wagon wheels have given me status as a healthy buck slave."

"Oh, I hate that word." America stepped back and put her hands up to her face. "That is what the slave traders use when they offer their male bondsmen for sale."

"Well, *we* do not have to think of ourselves as livestock, but most slaveholders do." Jerry paused and silently traced one of America's eyebrows and then he kissed it. "When Master Abraham comes to visit Master John, I will ask him for permission to marry. And I will bring up the subject of hiring me out to a landowner closer to this farm. It seems that my value as a slave would have gone up with my labor."

"Yes." America was still recovering from the thrill of the unexpected kiss.

"I must be on my way." He turned to leave the hemp shelter. "We will think of something. I have great hope that Master Abraham and your papa will support our marriage."

America followed him to the barn with a spring to her step despite the cold wind. It could not extinguish the warmth in her heart. She watched as Jerry patted the workhorse before leading it away from the barn and climbing on.

"Fare thee well! I hope to see you next Sunday!" They spoke the oft-used words together in harmony.

Chapter 28
Resolutions

AMERICA TIDIED THE HEMP HOUSE as she waited for Jerry. It had been her first opportunity to clean up their cozy corner of the building since they had been there in December in the peaceful quiet of the hemp field. Jeremiah had contracted America to be at the Tanner farm through Christmas to help when the extended family gathered for the big holiday dinner and festivities. Master Branch's turn had come again to host the big group.

Her time in Lexington before New Year day had been busy. She sewed a work dress of osnaburg fabric, and one of calico, a bib apron, and some nightclothes. Anne was there to enjoy her company and share America's excitement about marrying Jerry. No wedding plans were discussed because of the uncertainty about the owners' permission. Master John's attitude was troublesome and a stumbling block to Jerry's visitation privileges.

"Good afternoon, Merry." Jerry stood in the doorway of the hemp house. He had arrived sooner than usual and came out to the hemp field as a teasing surprise.

"Oh, Jerry! You startled me." America rushed into his arms. "Did you race over with your horse?"

"We just took advantage of the sunshine, dry fields, and temperate weather. The way seems to get shorter the more familiar we become with the trip each week. It is beautiful today. I have news about our marriage plans: some good, and some not so good."

"First, tell me about your mama. How is she?"

"She is doing tolerably well. Today, I left her sitting in the sunshine, crocheting a shawl for Mistress Lydia. She has crocheted since she was a child. It is amazing that she can manipulate the hook and yarn by feel in order to crochet, even though her sight is poor. I told her about our plans and she is curious to meet you."

"I would like to meet her, but I do not know if that will occur."

"Here is what I learned from Master Abraham. It seemed to me that he told what happened with Master John as a way to air his disappointment. He intended to negotiate a new contract to hire me out. He said that I was an experienced field hand now, and as I had grown in strength and abilities as a stockman, I was worth more. He proposed an increase in the hiring price for my labor. He also told Master John that I wish to marry and would require time away on Saturdays and Sundays. According to Master Abraham, Master John fussed and fumed. They talked and haggled and bargained. Finally, a compromise was reached. I will be allowed to come Saturday and Sunday every *other* week. The value of my contract will be higher."

"We will not have the benefit of married life as I imagined." America's scowl illustrated her frustration. *Whites rule black lives.*

"The contract will not take effect until next year, allowing Master John to negotiate hemp and livestock prices that should increase. That way, he will feel more secure paying a higher price for my hire." Jerry had to tell as much as he understood. "That is a disappointment too, Miss Merry. One that we should have known."

"At least the two of them recognize the value your work."

"Master Abraham hinted at a proposition that I might pursue and he would support," Jerry took on a hopeful look. "I could train Master Branch's young colts for use as carriage horses. I would hire myself out to Master Branch the two days every other week when I am here." He paused. "I will need to see if that time is sufficient to accomplish the training."

"Jerry, that sounds wonderful." America's outlook turned sunny, as it usually did when she was around Jerry. "I can see benefits all around, including the beginnings of a freedom nest egg."

"Merry, Merry." Jerry leaned in for a soft hug that warmed both of them. "I am sure Willie awaits in the barn."

"Yes, Mister Burns." America remembered she wanted to show Jerry a page in the songbook that Mistress Rebecca gave her four Christmases ago. "Remember the fabric covered songbook I keep with my nursery-rhyme book?"

"Yes. We have not looked at it much." He turned her around to head toward the barn. They shivered in the cold January wind.

"I look at it occasionally, searching for words I have learned in the Bible or rhyme book. It is nice to recognize old printed friends." Rushing into the shelter of the big building that housed warmth-producing animals and insulating straw and hay, America soon located her songbook. It was a wondrous Christmas gift from the Tanners her first year at Pleasant Green Hill.

"Jerry. Turn to song. . . Aahh." She had to stop to think the number. "I think it is 121."

"Yes." Jerry found it. "Faith's review and expectation," he read the heading on the page. Then his eyes traveled down the page to see the words. "Amazing grace. How sweet the sound." He looked up at the memory of the tune and sang a few notes.

"Yes!" America clapped her hands. "Amazing Grace! I know that song. I recognized the words because it is what Mama used to hum and sing as she ironed laundry clothes."

"You are on your way to being a full reader!" Jerry was enthusiastic about her ability to recognize the words all on her own.

America, more pleased with the heartfelt feelings that the words provided, wanted to share the song with Willie. "I will point to the words as we sing the song," she said.

Willie was surprised at the change in the proceedings that day. But he patiently listened as Jerry and America sang in perfect harmony, pointing to the words in the well-used fabric covered "Songs Part II" of *The Baptist Hymn Book*.

"Amazing grace! How sweet the sound! That sav'd a wretch like me./I once was lost, but now I'm found, was blind but now I see./' Twas grace that taught my heart to fear, and grace my fears reliev'd; /How precious did that grace appear, the hour I first believ'd./Through many dangers toils and snares, I have already come,/' Tis grace has brought me safe thus far, and grace will lead me home."

"I love that song." America closed the book and hugged it to her chest. "Harriet found this among the other hymn books at their church. Since it was only a part of a complete book, she asked the preacher if she could have it. She sewed a cover for it and then gave it to me for Christmas four years ago."

"It is a treasure for sure." Jerry cleared his throat, proud that he sang through the stanzas of the song with no difficulty. "Willie, have you worked on any reading since the holidays?"

"Mister Jerry." he nodded and smiled proudly, showing a striking resemblance to Henry. "Reuben showed me a paper book called *Harper's* that had a picture of Saint Nicholas and a poem about how he came down a chimney. He rode in a sleigh pulled by deer! I made out some of the words on the first page. It is a funny story. After he read the poem to me, Reuben had to put it away."

"We will just go over some of the words in the Bible story you and America already know."

The lesson began. America felt confident that the future would be brighter for her and Jerry when they married, despite the time restrictions in Jerry's contract. If he could hire himself out to Master Branch four days of the month, they could start a little freedom fund.

That outlook faded.

The next Sunday, Jerry quietly appeared in the barnyard, a distracted look on his face. As soon as America greeted him, he tended to the horse, and then took her elbow to steer her towards the hemp house.

"I do not know that it is a good idea to start a freedom nest egg, Merry." He came right to the point. His words fell flat and America knew from his sorrowful expression that sad news occupied his mind.

"I have been thinking about that." America smiled bravely and faced his frowning countenance. "The money would be for your freedom once we convince Papa that you would take care of me and he gave me free papers. When we purchase your freedom, we would both be free to raise our children outside of slavery's bonds." She thought her reasoning would comfort him.

"That is the trouble," was Jerry's quick response. "I read in Mister Crocket's newspapers that government officials ruled we would never be considered equal to whites." Jerry's voice strained as he told her that.

"What!" America immediately reacted. "You know that is not true!"

"A man in Missouri sued for his freedom because, as a slave, he had been hired out for many years, and before that had lived with his master in a state that prohibited slavery. He had accumulated enough money to buy his freedom but was always refused by one owner after another. What is most discouraging is that the chief judge in the national court wrote that people like you and me- descendants of Africans who were brought to this country as slaves-would never have rights as citizens because we are inferior to white people and not worthy to enjoy the same privileges."

"How did that come about?" America wanted to know the details.

"The newspaper is old, dated last April. It could be that Mister Crocket had not received it in the mail, or that Master John got hold of it to read himself. Lord knows, he would agree with the federal judges and their opinions. Maybe Master John wanted to see if anything applied to life here in Kentucky."

"Well, it is just discouraging. No matter how we work to better ourselves, the old attitudes are there: whites are superior to blacks. Color makes the difference."

"Yes, Merry. But, one circumstance is in our favor." Jerry wanted America to realize. "We now have the advantage of reading about what happens rather than hearing what the slave masters tell us."

"You are right, Jerry." America responded. "They could tell us anything they choose. Now, they cannot get away with that. We can reason and prepare our own lives and opinions according to what we read."

"I have decided not to try hiring myself out next year just to add money to the freedom fund. If the opportunity presents itself, I will be happy to work for a specific time and gain some money. But I do not want to tie myself down to responsibilities that would impose on my private time with you."

"Jerry, you are a dear. We will make do with what we have: always have, always will. That seems to be the lot we are given as slaves. Someday it will change. Aunt Dicy keeps telling me that we will have good times and bad."

"What carries me along is the understanding that we are just as smart as the white folk." Jerry turned toward the barn.

"We just have to prove our worth in a mannerly way-not out of hatred for what they think, but to show them we understand and enjoy many of the same things they do."

"Yes." Jerry squeezed America's waist and then walked with resolve toward Willie who was waiting at the barn door.

Chapter 29
Plans

AMERICA WOKE BRIGHT AND EARLY, looking forward to Jerry's Sunday visit. Then memory intruded. This month, January, was the beginning of his new contract. He would not be coming today, and instead would come Saturday and stay overnight the next weekend. *Aahh! I miss him already today. But I can look forward to his presence next Saturday and Sunday. And his overnight stay! How exciting!*

She went through her regular Sunday morning duties and helped prepare and serve Sunday dinner to the Tanner family as usual. *Perhaps I could work on the quilt after dinner, when the children were busy with their own Sunday afternoon activities.* The fabric pieces were spread on the slave cabin's floor, a distance from the fireplace hearth and out of the way of Aunt Dicy's rocking chair. Rose had indicated that she would not need any help until suppertime.

America sat in the sunbeam of the only window in the cabin to sew the squares together in the design she and Aunt Dicy fashioned. The elderly slave was napping. All was quiet and calm. America threaded her needle and arranged the fabric pieces in her hands to begin work on the quilt. *It will be so handsome when we get it finished.*

She heard the clopping of horse hooves in the barnyard. Opening the door of the cabin, she saw Jerry. *What a surprise! Had he forgotten his new contract? Not likely. Why is he here?*

"Oh, Jerry! How good to see you!"

"I am happy to be here, but things have changed." Jerry passed the reins back and forth between his hands as he explained. "Master John has renegotiated my contract with Master Abraham. He says the payment and my labor are to remain the same as it was because of the economic downturn in the markets. Those are the words he told me. He said that Master Abraham understood the fix he was in and, in order to help him get back on his feet, extended the present contract for another year."

"This means our wedding will be put on hold." America stated what she thought was obvious.

"Maybe not. We could still be married between Christmas and New Year." Jerry exhibited a determined look as he dismounted the horse and led it to the water trough. "It just means that we will not be enjoying those two days together every other week until next year." His frown was evident.

"I was looking forward to that." America matched Jerry's frown. "I just wonder how honest Master John is being. Could he be that unfortunate with the markets? Will the extra work time you provide him be necessary? Is the new contract worth more than he could handle?"

"I asked those same questions to myself on the way over." Jerry walked toward the slave cabin. He grimaced at the thought. "Master John could just be exerting his power over me. He must understand that I will obey his demands. This circumstance could be his way of showing a white superiority that I do not accept. He uses his family connections to get what he wants. At this time, the economic situation is not good. Mister Crocket's newspapers have shown that. Master Abraham hinted at it when I talked with him last year."

"There is not much we can do." America tried to talk herself into being positive.

"I truly think that Master Abraham wishes us well. Master John only looks out for his own interests and how much money he can make off the backs of slaves." Jerry looked around the barnyard. "Do you know where Willie is?"

"I told him that you would not be coming today, so I suspect he is off with Reuben. They were talking about making slingshots and target practicing." America looked shyly up to Jerry. "I will have you all to myself if Willie is not to be found."

"Looks like that. I do not mind at all." Jerry smiled. The workhorse nickered softly, a reminder that he needed some attention. As Jerry removed the saddle and led the horse into the barn, Henry appeared.

"Jerry. I understood you wouldn't be here today! Willie has gone off with Reuben looking for a good lilac bush or maple tree with suitable branches for slingshots." Henry motioned a direction away from the house.

"I must deliver a letter to Master Branch before I do anything else. Master John wrote to him about my visiting arrangement this year. I will be coming every Sunday afternoon as I had been. But next year should be different."

"I will see to it that Willie meets you on Sundays as usual. He seems to like the attention, and he is learning manners if nothing else."

America took up the conversation as Jerry went inside the house. "Willie likes the books. And he is not afraid to ask about a word that puzzles him. That shows he is taking charge of his own schooling."

When Jerry returned, he grabbed America's hand. "We will see you and Willie next week, Henry." They walked through the wide middle corridor of the barn, open at either end, and then outside toward the hemp field.

"The hemp house needs some attention. While we are tidying up there, we can discuss our wedding, and I can sew on our quilt." America always had a plan.

"All right, Miss Merry." Jerry squeezed her hand. "As your betrothed, I will see to it that our private quarters are suitable for habitation."

"Yes, Mister Jerry Burns."

Their goal was to shift the five hemp brakes, giving more room for a sitting area and bed. Each brake was at least five-feet long, three-feet wide and stood about three-feet tall. Moving the wooden machines took height and strength that America did not possess. Jerry did most of the dragging himself with America directing the maneuvers. They were exhausted by the time they had cleared an area for themselves, allowing for space needed for the field slaves to move each piece of equipment.

"Next month when they start hauling the brakes into the fields, we will see if our labor was sufficient. Seems we can fashion a bed in that corner where the straw bundles sit. We can do a little finishing work on that rough-hewn board and call it a table." Jerry wanted to make the hemp storage building seem livable.

"I will look around for something to serve as chairs." America's thoughts, though, were on fabric coverings for almost all the items Jerry had planned. Getting the quilt finished was her first priority, but she considered other things: a table cloth, sturdy chair coverings, a braided rug. Her experience in three different homes gave her ideas about how to make their quarters cozy despite the fact that they would be there only a short period every other week. Both of them viewed it as their first home-a refuge of love and safety.

"I will get some of the quilt pieces to work on now. Even though we have no fire for warmth, if we sit together close enough, we should be comfortable here." America was still overheated from the exertion of moving the hemp brakes.

"The sunshine is warmth enough for me." Jerry squinted heavenward.

When America returned she found that Jerry had repositioned the hemp straw bundles to take advantage of a sunbeam coming through the opening in the upper level of the building. The leftover hemp stalks and the wooden brakes warmed in the bright winter sunlight, made the area a snug haven.

America was full of questions, and she had answers ready for Jerry's consideration. "Where should we have our wedding? Will we need someone to lead the ceremony? Can your mama take part?"

"We should ask Master Branch if we could have it here, in his barn. Your papa would most likely have charge of the festivities. And Mama can ride here with Charles in Master John's carriage. I expect Master John and Mistress Lydia would come, so as to tout their status as landed gentry." Jerry listed answers to America's questions.

"We are of one mind." She had to comment on his statements. "This farm is the most likely, and the barn should still be clean from the Christmas doings. I think a few days after Christmas would be a good time for the celebration, and we would be starting life together as man and wife when the calendar turns to a new decade."

"It all sounds acceptable to me!" Jerry had rested enough from his labors with the hemp machines to be playful. "I can hardly wait for you to be my wife." He grabbed her around the waist and spun around. "There are many things we have no control over, but choosing a life partner was a gift from Lexington-the city, not the horse." He grinned at her questioning glance.

"What did Lexington, the city, have to do with choices?" America had to know.

"When we lived there, we encountered many people to associate with. Maybe me more than you. But…"

"I did not have many choices, Jerry. You, as a trusted male slave in a city, were able to move around, behave more like a free person, and meet many more people of all colors. I am restricted to my duties in a household. The only freedom I had in Lexington was to run a quick errand or walk from Papa's home to the Hunt Morgan house."

"You are correct, my love." Jerry gave a satisfied sigh. "In Lexington, you always faced the fear of being kidnapped and sold. Here, being kidnapped is only a slight worry, but the fear of abuse is present. With Henry's watchful eye, that has lessened, though."

"Yes, with your direction." America smoothed her dress. "You were thinking that, in Lexington, we each decided on our own to start a friendship. We were not commanded to form a bond. Papa would never have chosen you to be my husband. I do not know if he even considered the possibility. But he approves of you and thinks you are a good match for me. I have heard that some slaves have no choice of partners, that they are put together like breeding animals." She shuddered.

"In Lexington, we found each other. Even though it took Master Morgan's interest in Walter Scott to bring us together, I want to think that, sooner or later, we would have paired up."

"Amazing grace." America nodded. "That is what tied us to each other." She paused. "It is also the best song I know. I will ask Papa if he would read the words from my songbook when he leads the ceremony."

"Now, you intend to put words in his mouth?" Jerry teased.

"Those are not my words, but I love what they say and how they are put together." Being more practical, America steered the conversation back to wedding plans. "Here are a few more thoughts on our doings. The quilt could be put up for the gathering like a wall hanging. That is, if I get it done in time. Do you realize it is a connection from your mama, my mama, and Aunt Dicy? They each have had a say in its construction. Is that an acceptable arrangement?"

"Oh, yes, Merry." Then Jerry turned to her with a twinkle in his eye. "When will it be taken down for its intended use? I hope to be under it with you that night!"

"We will be Merry and Jerry Burns then. Oh, happy night!"

"I must be on my way before I get more ideas about taking part in our marriage." Jerry giggled at the thought and then became very solemn. "Today has been wondrous. The sunshine just heightened my glad spirits. Working with you all this afternoon has just added more reasons we should be together for life."

"Without a doubt."

They walked arm in arm along the fence to the barn. America secured the needle to her quilt pieces and folded them into her apron as she waited for Jerry to saddle up the workhorse. After a quick hug and kiss, he turned the horse toward the lane.

"Fare thee well! I hope to see you next Sunday!"

Chapter 30
Beginning

DECEMBER 28, 1859, WAS A DAY AMERICA would remember for the rest of her life. The household of Pleasant Green Hill farm bustled with friends and family who came to celebrate her marriage to Jerry. Jeremiah and Anne arrived first in the finest livery brougham, a suitable advertisement for the Murphy business. Uncle Eli came in another Murphy Livery carriage, transporting Cook and Aunt Bette in the back. Jerry came with Daniel and Hannah and Master Abraham in a Morgan family brougham. Jerry's brother Charles had driven the Skillman horse-drawn carriage to bring their mama and Master and Mistress John Skillman to the festivities.

The Tanner family hosted the gathering, which would take place in the barn. Master Branch and Mistress Rebecca stood at the wide entrance to the barn to greet and shake hands with visitors as they arrived. Harriet and Sarah saw to the needs of the female guests, while Reuben and David were on duty to attend to male guests. Rose and Nina busied themselves with food preparations and were assisted by Cook and Aunt Bette, who carried in a modestly decorated fruitcake from the renowned Hunt Morgan kitchen, a smaller version of one that was served at Hannah and Daniel's wedding.

Anne brought a waistcoat she had designed and sewed for Jerry. On the lapels, she had embroidered turquoise flowers with green vines and leaves that matched America's two-piece dress. Jerry immediately recognized the match as he pulled on the vest-like garment. America, glowing in her blue-green dress set, sneaked a quick kiss to his cheek.

Henry and Willie had tidied up the barn and hung the now-completed quilt above the wagon that, cleaned up and covered with a cloth, served as a viands table. The wedding cake presided over all the toothsome refreshments and fruit drinks. A brand-new broom that Henry and Aunt Dicy made leaned against the wagon.

"Ladies and gentlemen." Jeremiah raised his voice. "Please gather in front of this splendid wagon table to see and hear what you all have come to witness."

America took Jerry's arm and stood in front of her papa. To rid himself of the anxiety of speaking before the mixed group of black and white, slave and free, rich and poor, Jeremiah repeated the revised nursery rhyme. "Merry, Merry, not contrary, how does your garden grow?"

America answered in a clear voice, "With silver bells, and magic spells, and bright colors all in a row!" She looked around at the assembled friends and relatives, at the warm surroundings, and finally rested her eyes on Jerry.

"Before we hear the vows," Jeremiah pulled a fabric-covered book out of the breast pocket of his dark wool suit coat. It was America's songbook, the Christmas gift from the Tanners. Turning to page 121, he continued, "I wish to read the words of America's favorite song." He cleared his throat. "Amazing grace, how sweet the sound, that sav'd a wretch like me. I once was lost, but now I'm found, was blind but now I see." Encouraged by the nods and murmurs of approval, he continued through all six stanzas. Anne bowed her head and rhythmically followed his words.

"And, now here is what we came for." He turned to Jerry. "Do you take America to be your wife?"

"Yes, sir!" Jerry did not hesitate.

"America, will you have Jerry as your husband?"

"I will, Master Murphy!" America could not suppress the happiness in her voice.

"I now pronounce you husband and wife unless death or distance part you."

"Amazing grace." America looked at Jerry.

"Yes, Merry. You have it. How sweet the sound!" was his reply.

Anne softly began to hum the song. Members of the group joined in until everyone was either quietly singing or humming the favorite hymn. The moment turned into a thanksgiving and hopeful respect for the lives of Jerry and Merry. Aunt Dicy solemnly placed the handle of the new broom in Jeremiah's hands, as she kept hold of the straw bristle end.

"They ain't married 'til the broom says so!" Henry shouted, breaking the earnestness of the occasion. Everyone laughed in relief.

Aunt Dicy and Jeremiah laid the new broom on the barn floor and motioned America and Jerry to come forward to stand between them. Jeremiah directed. "At the count of three, jump over the broom!"

Jerry squeezed his arms tightly around America's waist. Jeremiah raised his hands to signal to the gathered company. They counted together, "One! Two! Three! Jump!"

They did.

"I again pronounce you husband and wife unless death or distance part you." Jeremiah smiled. "My friend London Ferrill used to say those words, so I will just repeat them for him."

Everyone clapped, which startled the horses. The ensuing talk, shouts, and laughter of the guests drowned out the stamps and neighing and squeals of the equines. Soon all in attendance, horses and humans, settled down to the business of enjoying the afternoon and evening.

Jerry's mama met America, who invited her over to sit and visit with Anne and Aunt Dicy. Sewing was the main topic of conversation as they inspected the quilt. Jerry introduced Henry and Willie to Master John and Mistress Lydia Skillman, hinting of other servants at Willow Valley farm.

Harriet was thrilled that the songbook she had discovered was utilized that day. She sat down to flip through the pages searching for other favorite songs. Sarah, full of sweet fruitcake, interrupted her sister to investigate the new broom. "Let us go jump the broom. Is it a magic thing?" They placed it on the floor and jumped. Sarah looked around: no flying carpet, nothing disappeared, no glass slipper.

"Well sister, I guess when they jump together it is like they are partners and need to sweep out a place to live." Harriet tried to make sense of the popular slave ceremony.

"That is what America and Jerry have been doing with the hemp house." Sarah paused. "He is nice. I know she loves him. Maybe the broom jump is magic just for them."

Married life was magic for America and Jerry despite the restrictions that slavery placed on them. Their son, Isaac who was born just a year and six days after the wedding, came into this world January 1, 1861. Isaac's birthday was the same as the designated foaling date of the thoroughbreds he rode to fame and fortune. A source of merriment and pride, he was amazing.

If it was written, America could have read and recited another modified version of the old nursery rhyme: "Jerry, Jerry, not contrary, how does your Isaac grow?"

"With love that dwells where freedom swells, and slavery begins to slow."

AFTERWORD

AMERICA DIED IN 1879, SO SHE DID NOT ENJOY her son Isaac's celebrity in the thoroughbred racing world, which came in the 1880s and 1890s. But she started him on that path, taking advantage of her association with trainer Eli Jordan and the household of horse owner James Williams.

Thoroughbred racing was a favorite leisure time activity of the rich and powerful. Landed gentry owned the best racetracks, the most prosperous farms, the prized horses, and, back then, the slaves themselves who toiled with those possessions. Triumph at the track was accomplished in the capable hands of their slaves, and, after emancipation, by their lowly paid black servants.

A newspaper article in the July 29, 1891 edition of the *Kentucky Leader* led to research that resulted in this historical fiction story. Eli Jordan was a friend of the Murphy family. Having taught America's son Isaac his first lessons in horsemanship, he described America and Isaac. The title of the article was *Ike Murphy's Real Name.*

"Ike's mammy lived at my home in Lexington for a great many years. [She] was a Murphy, and when about twenty years of age she married a man named Burns. When the little fellow had grown strong enough to hold a bridle he was taught and trained to ride. No, his name is not Isaac Murphy, as almost every lover of race horses supposes, but it is Isaac Burns. The reason he took the name of Murphy was because he was so requested by his mother, who desired that her son ride under the name of her father. This request was made for the reason that the old granddaddy was proud of Isaac and had great hopes of his future as a jockey. [But] few now know that the rich and great rider is the same little yellow Ike Burns who rode in unimportant races about Lexington and Louisville twenty years ago."

ABOUT THE AUTHOR

CATHY MOORE, A RESIDENT OF KENTUCKY, was inspired to write *Hired Out* from her experience as a tour guide at the Kentucky History Center and her fascination with thoroughbred horse racing through her employment as a Keeneland Library assistant.

After graduating from Earlham College in Indiana, she began her professional career as an elementary school teacher and librarian in Illinois. She and husband Don moved to New Orleans and lived not far from the Fair Grounds Race Course where they delved into the culture, history, and practices of horse racing. They moved to Kentucky and immersed themselves in the thoroughbred milieu. Imagining the challenges of a bi-racial girl in antebellum Kentucky, Cathy researched and wrote the story of America Murphy, an actual native of the city of Lexington. *Hired Out* is a visualization of America's life as a slave living in a border state, across the Ohio River from freedom. America touches history through her later connections with the racing world.